LAP 121

---

a novel by

ROBERT LOUIS DIGIACOMO

REVERIE PUBLISHING

LAP 121

Published by Reverie Publishing LLC / August 2008
Wesley Chapel, Florida

This is the work of fiction. Names, characters, places and incidents are either the product of the author's imagination or are used fictitiously. Any resemblance to persons living or dead as well as locations and events is coincidental.

No classified information was used to create this book, and no member of any government agency was contacted in researching this book.

Library of Congress Control Number: 2008907246

ISBN-13: 978-0-6152-3991-0

www.lap121.com
www.reveriebooks.com

Printed in the United States of America.

LAP 121

PROLOGUE

FEBRUARY 21ST

AS WITH THE WORLD TRADE CENTER attack, the luck was with the terrorists that day. Nouri couldn't have known the men would hijack a tanker truck, which had three compartments separating the different grades of fuel. The driver said his prayers— screamed, "*Allāhu Akbar*", and pushed a speed dial button to detonate the charge.

In a span of milliseconds, several things happened. The initial explosion caused the steel bulkheads between the compartments to expand outward, rupturing each end of the tanker. A spray of raw fuel was blown out with such intensity that it was propelled hundreds of feet in the air. When the fuel ignited, the explosion was horrendous with a fireball that reached nearly a half-mile-high. The grandstand's top level including the VIP tower crashed onto the racetrack. Those seated in the lower deck near the blast who were not vaporized were cut into ribbons by the sharp fragments from the metal bleachers.

In the next second, the pressure wave extended sideways killing most people within 1,000 yards of the tower. Seconds later heat from the unexploded, burning gasoline elevated temperatures to nearly 1,200 degrees. Race cars slammed into the upper deck, which was now lying across the track. Burning wreckage rained down on the infield spectators, causing more fires. Pit row and the garage area were now ablaze and noxious clouds of burning chemicals filled the air.

High above, the airship's pilot and crew watched in astonishment. The winds aloft had pushed the craft out of position, and they were returning to the track area when the explosion erupted. They watched a mushroom cloud form that reached nearly a half mile above their present altitude. They surely would have crashed had they been on station.

As Nouri Naderi had predicted, the airship was broadcasting a live TV signal to the local affiliate who beamed it to a satellite. All over the nation millions of people who were watching *The Great American Race* were mesmerized. This was reality television in the extreme. The aircraft cameras showed people on fire or being crushed to death as the stampedes tried to make their way out to the parking lot only to be met by burning and exploding cars. Similar carnage was everywhere. International Speedway Boulevard was impassable, laden with wrecked cars and carnage that filled the street.

The airship crew filmed until the sun finally set about 6:00 pm hiding from the cameras much of the horror that was still unfolding. By now helicopters from all the major networks had arrived. Many beamed their powerful searchlights on the speedway grounds show- ing macabre vignettes of the devastation. The talking heads reported that help had not yet arrived. The scene was one of chaos and suffering.

1

EIGHT MONTHS EARLIER

MOST WOMEN AND SOME MEN would call her attractive, but Beth did nothing to make herself look younger or prettier. Special Agent Elizabeth Anne Cuddy, named after her maternal grandmother, was 37 years old, physically fit, occasionally demanding and frequently impatient. She quickly became annoyed as she watched her new partner navigate through the maze of cubicles on his way to their work area. She understood that breaking in new people meant hundreds of questions and endless hours of listening to war stories about their crime-fighting prowess, something she had endured several times in her 12 years with the FBI. Today she was anxious to get the process moving.

"Hey, where's mine?" Beth said as she looked down at the cup Mark was carrying.

"Oh, I'm sorry did you want one? I can go back to the coffee machine." Here he was on the first minute of the first day, ready to impress, but already violating some rule of unit etiquette. Beth smiled, "I've already had mine." She was a one-cup-a-day person who had far too much energy for a caffeine habit. Beth was also one of those rare morning people, a trait she realized would frequently cause dismay among many of her colleagues. She hoped that Mark would not be one of them.

"Ready to get started?" she asked.

They would share a large cubicle that housed several computers, each equipped with multiple monitors. Their seating arrangement was back-to-back, but they could roll their chairs around to work side-by-side if needed—and this was one of those occasions.

Mark Siene had arranged his work space over the weekend. He had introduced himself to Beth the previous Friday when he reported for his new assignment in the Counterterrorism section for the FBI's Jacksonville field office. Mark had only been with the Bureau for six years, and this was a big step up. He knew the FBI allocated most of its funding to this area, and the unit was equipped with all the latest and greatest tech toys to fight the *evil doers*, as a former president used to call them.

"Roll your chair over here", Beth said. "Did they give you a password on Friday?"

"Yup, I'm all set."

"Have you heard rumors about our new system?"

"No not really," Mark answered.

"Good! That means that our security is working, well hopefully. I'm already signed-in to my queue on this monitor. Look over here." She pointed to the smaller of the two displays, sitting on her desk. "This is part of the new Threat Identification and Classification System or T.I.C.S. You'll hear most people here calling it *ticks*." She said, watching Mark smile. "And before you say it—no, the system wasn't buggy when we installed it."

"As with each team of agents, we're assigned a number of people that appear on the new National Counter Terrorism Center Database."

"About how many people are in the system?" Mark asked.

"I would guess more than a hundred thousand. The Bureau initially assigns most agent teams about 750 people, but it tends to grow over time. Right now we have about 900 people to monitor. We look for unusual activities."

"That seems like a lot of people for us to watch." Mark said, sounding somewhat concerned.

"Not really. We don't get new information on each subject everyday. See our queue has thirteen items in it today. When you sign-in, you'll see an identical list, which has to be worked by each of us separately within 48 hour window. That way we're sure that nothing gets missed." She pointed to the large 32-inch monitor as she clicked on the first item, "Watch this."

On the screen what looked to Mark like an old fashioned cork bulletin board appeared with items attached to it. There were thumbnail representations of photos, letters, notes and other icons.

"It looks like a corkboard," Mark said.

"That's what some agents call it. Watch as I click on each little picture. If it's a photo or piece of correspondence of some kind, the item enlarges and an image appears like this," Beth said as she choose what looked to Mark like a tiny e-mail.

"What's the little red symbol in the corner?"

"You'll like this. If you push the right mouse button when you're over the symbol, an English translation will appear. The same thing happens when you select a transcript of a telephone call. You can actually listen to the original call, if you want."

"Really?"

"To be honest, that function is almost worthless."

"Why?" Mark asked.

"Unless, you speak five or so languages, it doesn't help."

"What's that icon there?"

"That's video surveillance footage. If you double-click the symbol while the video is running another screen pops-up to show you a satellite image of the area where the video was shot, and even a topographical map, if you want it. You can also do that with the phone calls."

"Nice," Mark said, impressed.

"You'll see that it does a whole lot more as you work with it," she said as her cell phone rang. The caller ID showed it was from her father. She didn't mind him calling her at work. That's where she spent most of her time now, anyway. She said to Mark, "I'm gonna take this. Why don't you sign-in and review some of the items in our queue. The flashing thumbnails—that's the new information.

Her father always made it a point to call her several times a week when he was back in Maine. He spent winters with Beth after her husband, a Special Forces Ranger, was killed in Afghanistan. She talked with him for a while, mostly about the house he was helping her remodel, then about her sister and her sister's children.

After she finished, she went back to Mark. She noticed he had filled a whole page with questions. "I see you need some answers."

"Does all this information come from covert operations?"

"I would think not. As you work with the system more, you'll see that much of it is open source intelligence. Somewhere in our government, computers are scanning newspapers, websites and other places for information."

"How do they determine who gets on our list?" Mark asked.

"I don't actually know," Beth responded.

Her answer impressed Mark. In the past he found that many senior special agents wouldn't admit they didn't know something and evaded the issue, or worse yet, would come up with that tired old line: *If I told you, I'd have to kill you.* He had heard that at least a hundred times a year.

"I've noticed that almost everyone in our queue has some sort of Florida connection, though. Other than that, I don't know. Why don't we go ahead and work one of these together, and I'll show you," Beth said as the monitor displayed information about Nouri Naderi.

2

———

IT WAS SUMMER IN CANADA. The four young
men didn't work much in the summer. They preferred to ride their motorcycles as much as possible.
They had just arrived back at the old garage after joining several other members of their motorcycle club on a
trip to the Niagara Falls area about 85 miles away. The
new passport rules were a pain, but they frequently
crossed into the States where motorcycle parts were
sometimes cheaper. Now, Nouri Naderi sat with his
two friends and his brother in the old masonry building
that formerly served as both office and garage for his
grandfather's trucking company. Nowadays it was the
official clubhouse for the Scimitars, the only all-Muslim
motorcycle club in Canada.

The trucking company had outgrown its former pre-
mises long ago, but the building was still in good repair.
It was located in an industrial section of town, and
shared it's roadway with several factories, gas stations

and other small businesses. The Naderi family held on to the property because the real estate values continued to increase in the area.

The original office could accommodate eight or nine people and had a private area once used by Nouri's grandfather. Most of the employee furniture was long gone and in its place were hand-me-down lounge chairs and old leather sofas. They turned the private spaces into a video game area. A very large flat screen monitor now sat on a long low table.

The garage part of the old building no longer contained fuel trucks but was full of motorcycles. Some of the club's members—there were 13 in all—kept their bikes there.

The four Canadian born Iranians had another thing in common besides motorcycles. They hated the *States*, as many Canadians were fond of calling the United States. For Nouri and his brother, Sami, this animosity was due largely to their family's experience. Amir Naderi, their grandfather, was both a devote Shiite Muslim and business man. He had lost everything when he was exiled in 1953 along with hundreds of others after the Shah of Iran was returned to power by the United States. He managed to reach Canada after almost being killed during the coup. He eventually settled in southern Ontario, near Toronto, where he felt there was opportunity for him and his family. He turned out to be right. The company he started had grown to over thirty fuel tanker trucks and was now worth millions. In spite of his success, he never forgave America for its role in making him leave his homeland,

and he made sure this hatred was passed down to his grandsons.

The Naderi's family animosity, though, didn't stop Nouri from choosing America as the place to get his college education. He barely graduated from the University of South Florida in Tampa, majoring in chemical engineering. His younger brother, as he often did, was following Nouri's lead. Sami Naderi currently attended USF, studying electrical engineering. Nouri and Sami Naderi didn't know it, but this was how they managed to get themselves on the FBI's watch list.

For several years, the FBI had undercover agents on campus stemming from accusations that a USF professor was raising funds for terrorist organizations. Later, an incident involving two students accused of plotting an attack on a United States military installation increased their interest. The Bureau took no chances. If you attended the University, and had an Arab or Persian name, you landed on the list. Apparently this was how Nouri and later his brother Sami came to the FBI's attention.

Now, the four young men sat in the building talking and drinking sodas from the old refrigerator that occupied a corner of the office-turned-clubhouse. Their religious training prohibited them from drinking alcohol, including beer.

The usual clubhouse conversation would generally move from motorcycles, to video games to another favorite topic—blowing things up in America. This day was no different. One of their favorite video games was the same flight simulation that the 9/11 terrorists used to plan their attack on New York City. The young men would frequently take turns flying into the World Trade Center—a location that was still on the older version of the game.

"Instead of trying to knock down some building, I'd go for a bigger body count, like crashing into a stadium during Super Bowl or the World Series or something," said Farid. "Somewhere where there's a live TV camera."

"If you blew up a stadium, wouldn't you take out the TV cameras?" Reza asked trying to sound intelligent.

Farid Danesh had the bad habit of calling his younger brother stupid in front of people, and Reza was always trying to prove him wrong, which was at best, a waste of time.

"No, at the big events they usually have a blimp hovering over the stadium," answered Farid.

"Good point, I guess," Reza said to his brother. "But those events call for extra security and the Americans have probably already thought of an attack from the air."

Nouri said, "You know, when I was going to school in Florida I saw that blimp in the air both times I went to the Daytona 500 races in February. There had to be 100,000 people there, and the speedway is right next to a main airport for the city. I've also seen that blimp over Disney World in Orlando. But I think Disney wouldn't be a good target; it's too spread out."

"That many people go to NASCAR races?" asked Reza

"Yeah, it's huge."

"So you've been to the Speedway a couple times, aye?" asked Farid.

"More than that. I told you about the motorcycle races they have every March during Bike Week. I went to that three times. It's at the same place. Remember, I always tried to get you guys to visit me during that time of the year?"

"Right, who had money for plane tickets?" answered Farid.

"I would've sent you the money, aye."

"Hey guy, you got money now, but you didn't have it back then. I remember paying for the pizza when you were home on holiday," said Farid. "By the way, what are you putting in that computer?"

"Just some things we're talking about," replied Nouri, not caring for Farid's tone.

"Are you stupid?" Farid asked. There was no mistaking his tone.

"I told you, don't call me stupid. You can save that for your brother," Nouri shot back.

"Hey . . ." Reza said.

Farid shouted, "That's how those twelve guys got arrested in Mississauga a few years ago. Remember, they got themselves picked up for that bogus terrorist plot. The Mounties found a bunch of stuff on their laptops."

Sami, Nouri's brother who was home for the summer, and had been quiet up to now, said, "Come on guys."

Sami knew his older brother Nouri wasn't stupid. He did graduate from college with a chemical engineering

degree, but his brother sometimes showed poor judgment. This was one reason he knew his father, who was
now managing the company since their grandfather fell
ill and later died, wasn't grooming him to take over. He
had relegated Nouri's role to that of safety officer. Sami
once heard his father tell his mother that he couldn't do
much harm in that area. Nouri didn't seem to care. One
time he told Sami, he thought he was overpaid for what
he was doing anyway. Nouri had a lot of free time. As
company safety office, he traveled to five distribution
terminals located throughout southern Ontario. Since
he reported to no one but his father, nobody questioned
his whereabouts on a daily basis. Certainly, the terminal
managers didn't complain about his lack of looking
over their shoulders. It appeared to Sami that everyone
seemed happy with the arrangement.

Sami knew Nouri's main interest was in their motorcycle club. He was president of the Scimitars, named
after the long curved blade Persian warriors used to
carry. Acceptance into the club was simple. A person
had to be male, a practicing Muslim, have a full beard,
drive like a maniac and ride a streetfighter sport bike.
The streetfighter usually started life off as a Japanese or
British built motorcycle, then modified by first removing the fairings to show its mechanical workings and
making a number of other changes. Sami knew that in
the case of Nouri's bike, Farid did the work. He was
very good at converting the high-powered sport bikes
into streetfighters. He installed aftermarket exhaust
cans, heavy-duty shock absorbers, big brake disks, new
calipers and other parts to make Nouri's bike go faster,

stop quicker and look meaner. Farid used the old garage to perform these modifications on most of the other club members' bikes, as well. Sami knew he needed the money because Farid Danesh and his brother Reza did not come from a well-to-do family. Their father worked for an import/export company and made frequent trips back to Iran. The elder Danesh had moved to Canada during the Iran-Iraqi War in 1984. He made no secret of the fact that he hated the United States because he felt that America had backed Iraq against his home country. Sami knew that several Danesh family members were killed in that war from a poison gas attack by Iraq. He overheard Aram frequently tell his sons that America was responsible for the family deaths.

Sami Naderi's father had given both Danesh brothers a job. They worked part-time cleaning and filling company tanker trucks. They had not attended college or furthered their education after high school in any way except for their continued studies of the Koran. Frequently, they griped to Sami, Nouri or anyone else who would listen about the lack of opportunities in Canada. Of course, in their minds, this had little to do with their lack of ambition. They preferred to blame it on the United States, taking their lead from some Canadian politicians and media pundits who claimed that Canada's North American brother to the south, big-footed their economy. True or not, Sami knew that his two friends bought totally into the argument, which added to their dislike for the United States.

Along with Sami and his brother, Farid and Reza

were serious about their religion. They currently attended a Mosque where the Imam preached a fundamentalist anti-western type of Islam. The cleric would frequently use America and Israel as a symbol of all that was wrong with the world. So, it was no surprise that with their family's history and their religious zeal, the young men were fast becoming radicalized.

3

"**M**ARK, SEE THE ITEM that's highlighted. That's the new information. Let's look at it," said Beth.

A list of names appeared with a note that explained that this was a membership roster from the *Markaz al Islami* mosque in Toronto, known for its radicalism.

"How come we received this today?" asked Mark.

"One of the names on the list matches our subject, Nouri Naderi. It may be the same guy, but not necessarily. If this subject had a higher threat level code we'd probably want to investigate further."

"What's a threat level code?" asked Mark.

"That's this number right here. We've assigned our friend Nouri here a level one. The range is one through ten. Currently only one individual in the world is assigned a ten."

"Let me guess. Would that be Bin Laden?" Mark asked.

"That's right. Even though we looked at this one to-gether, you still have to process it on your own com-puter. One of us must do the first review within 24 hours, and we both have to look at it within 48. If neither of those things happen, our assistant special agent in charge of Counterterrorism finds the item in her queue. The ASAC hates that."

"What are those names at the bottom?"

"Apparently, the list of mosque members also con-tains names that another team of agents is monitoring—the names at the bottom. Sometimes this sends up a red flag. It's a connect-the-dots thing. Later you may want to e-mail the other team to see if something is going on with their subjects," said Beth.

"How would we go about investigating further if they thought something was going on?"

"For one thing, you could click on this symbol here which notifies NSA to begin eavesdropping on Naderi's calls and to monitor his Internet activity. By the way, that automatically happens on level five threats and above."

"Don't we need a court order?"

"It depends. The rules aren't as clear-cut as you may be used to. Over here, we deal with the Patriot Act and FISA. When you were at Quantico for training, you may recall the discussion on the 1978 Foreign Intelligence Surveillance Act. When I was there, they told us that it requires a warrant to intercept international communi-cations which involve anyone in the United States. It also requires a warrant to eavesdrop on communica-tions between foreigners that go through computers here in the United States. Beth pointed at the large monitor, "See right here? Nouri Naderi is a Canadian citizen who lives in Canada, so in my opinion a warrant isn't needed for phone or other taps."

"What do you, mean other taps?"

"In certain cases we now have the ability to monitor someone's web-browsing activity."

"You're kidding me. How is that even possible?"

"I don't know, but that's what this symbol does. Press the right mouse button, and you can choose from a listing of time-frames from one day to five years. It's similar to the history file on your home computer, only this is for someone else's activity," said Beth.

"That's pretty incredible."

Beth went on, "It's legal now since the Patriot Act was passed, but it requires a warrant from the FISA court if it's a U.S. citizen. To be safe, we ask for a warrant on everybody."

"So you would ask for one on Nouri here?"

"Yeah, why make it a judgment call? The FISA court grants the warrants nearly every time we ask. Besides, that's the way Sheryl wants it."

A voice from behind them said, "How are you getting on, Mark?"

Beth hated it when Sheryl Niblock, the ASAC, snuck up behind her. She was always doing that, and it aggravated Beth to no end. They turned to face Sheryl and Mark said, "Pretty good."

"Beth, my wish is that you get Mark up to speed on TICS as soon as possible," said Sheryl.

Beth smiled thinking of her ex-partner, now retired, who used to say that Sheryl was the most manipulative person he had ever met who found almost any occasion to use the most manipulative phase in the English language, "My wish is . . ."

"So Mark, have any questions?" asked Sheryl.

"Actually one; how are we able to monitor someone's web-browsing activity?"

Sheryl turning to walk away said, "That information is classified and on a need-to-know basis. I'd tell ya', but then I'd have to kill ya'."

Mark winced.

4

SHERYL NIBLOCK, the assistant special agent in charge, had been in a foul mood all morning. Her clothes felt tight, and as she sat there working through the items in the TICS system, she was becoming more and more uncomfortable. She never had a weight problem before. She didn't eat all that much, but she was drinking quite a bit of wine lately. That might be part of the cause for her discomfort, she thought. Sheryl knew that she should exercise more. There was even a health club in the building, but she was too tired to exercise after work. The few times each month she did get up early enough to go to the club, she would always see Beth running on the treadmill. Sheryl could barely do 20 minutes on the elliptical machine, and Beth would be running when she got there, and still running when she left. One of the trainers mentioned that Beth usually ran at least five miles almost every day. This was one reason for Sheryl's animosity toward Beth.

Although Sheryl Niblock did a good job hiding it, she couldn't stand Beth Cuddy. She had the impression that Beth thought she was better than she was. It was worse when Beth's ex-partner still worked in the unit. They would team up and make her feel like she was somehow beneath them. She thought to herself, well, he's gone and I'm still here.

All morning Sheryl had put off her least favorite chore—working with that damn TICS system. There must be two hundred items in her queue, she reckoned, and that really pissed her off. Besides reviewing those items where people missed the 48-hour window, she also had to handle the *second look* when her people went on vacation or didn't have a partner. For the last month, she'd been doing that for Ms. Cuddy. However, there was no 48-hour clock on her, which was the only thing that made the whole process tolerable.

After about fifty items, Sheryl had enough. It was such a chore. In her mind, the real job was to protect high value targets in her district. The Jacksonville office covered all of north Florida, going as far south as the Kennedy Space Center. She also had the entire panhandle including Tallahassee and Pensacola and all points in between. This included six military bases and four major airports. Her job also included meeting with local government leaders; she would reassure mayors, legislators and the like that the FBI was on top of things in their districts. She liked this part of the job—meeting with politicos. That is except for today.

Another reason for her foul mood was that she had a meeting this afternoon with Milton Fryer, the mayor of

Daytona Beach—another person she disliked. Milton was a *toucher* and Sheryl couldn't stand to be touched. However, that didn't stop her from placing her hand lightly on someone's forearm or shoulder when she tried to charm them. Another thing about Milton was he was always quoting Bible verses. Before he had become mayor, Milton had been pastor of the largest Baptist church in Volusia County, and Sheryl had no use for religion. Her parents made her attend a parochial school all the way through the twelfth grade. Any closeness to God she felt was driven out of her by the nuns of her youth.

Sheryl managed to get through another 60 items during the next hour. She moved as fast as she could—only giving a cursory glance to many entries. She had agents to do the analysis, and she was sure they were conscientious in their scrutiny.

The phone rang and caller ID said it was her real estate agent. She was trying to sell her condominium and wasn't having much luck. Her agent was bugging her to lower the price, which she had resisted up to now. Sheryl never really liked the place. The only reason she bought it was her former boss lived there. She figured when it was time for promotions or reviews, it would be harder for him to overlook her or give her a less than stellar evaluation if he had to see more of her everyday. She even made friends with his wife, Helene, who was a real cow. This strategy seemed to work because he recommended her for his old job as Assistant Special Agent in Charge of the Counterterrorism Section when he left. Of course, it also could have been because she had walked up behind him as he referred to her as a "split-tail" to one of his cronies. This was a derogatory term used by some older agents for their new women colleagues. Both she and Beth's ex-partner were up for the position and she got it. So now, she didn't need the condo.

Sheryl let the call go to voice mail and headed for the one available bureau car that was in the parking garage. Thank God, the person who used it last had the good sense to park the sedan in a shady spot. It was June in Jacksonville, and it was hot and muggy. Although she had spent most of her adult life in Florida, she wasn't a big fan of the sun or the heat. For a Florida resident she was quite pale.

She was running a little late, so she phoned Mayor Fryer. She would be meeting him and the police and fire chiefs who headed the first response teams for any incidents. A representative of local Home Land Security would also be there. Today they all would tour the Daytona International Speedway grounds, which was arguably the highest profile target in the area, second only to the International Airport.

After Milton Fryer's assistant put the call through, she said, "Hello Mr. Mayor, I'm running a little late, the traffic's terrible." This wasn't true, but she thought he wouldn't know the difference. "My wish would be that we could meet at the racetrack in about two hours." The mayor agreed, so they arranged a time and convenient meeting spot. Daytona International Speedway was about 90 miles away from her office, which was located on the southeast side of Jacksonville in a modern office park. Without traffic, the ride was less than two hours because the Speedway was just off I-95, north of the I-4 interchange.

Sheryl phoned her real estate agent who didn't have much good news. She thought about the great house Beth Cuddy had, located right on the St. John's River. Beth referred to it as a *fixer-upper*. Sheryl was there once for a barbecue on Fourth of July, and the place looked like something you would see in a magazine. The last thing Sheryl said to her realtor was, "My wish would be that you guys could be much more aggressive in your marketing effort. I don't think we have to lower the price."

5

WHEN SHERYL ARRIVED at the Speedway, she walked into the visitor's center and spotted the men talking to someone she hadn't met. After shaking hands all around, the police chief introduced her to the speedway manager. He was a nice looking man and didn't hold her hand too long while shaking it like Milton Fryer was fond of doing.

The manager said, "Let me give you some background, then we can take a tour. As you know, the speedway hosts a number of major events throughout the year beginning in February with the Daytona 500, or *The Great American Race*, as the fans and media tend to call it. We have other major auto and motorcycle races all year long as well as other venues. The Speedway sits on 430 acres and we have seats for about 168,000 fans. During a major race like the Daytona 500, over 200,000 people are usually on the property. Agent Niblock, did you notice the length of the grandstands when you entered the grounds?"

"Yeah, they go a long way," she replied remembering that as she looked for the visitor's center, they did seem to go on forever.

The manager went on, "Most of the seating here at the Speedway is along the front stretch, which is about 3,000 feet. The grandstand area is more than a half a mile long with a tower area in the middle housing an upper deck."

"How long is the racetrack?" the person from Homeland Security asked.

"It depends on the race, but The Daytona 500 circuit is two and half miles, which translates to 200 laps around the track."

"How long does the race take?" asked Sheryl.

"It depends on a number of factors, but what I think you may be asking is—how long will the 200,000 race fans be on the property. If that is your question, then I would say a long time. Most fans arrive about 11:00 in the morning and leave after 7:00 in the evening."

Sheryl turned to the Police Chief and asked, "What kind of security do we have here?"

"Well, besides the security personnel the track provides, we call in our reserve officers. Daytona Beach is used to big events like Bike Week, which draws 250,000 motorcyclists, and other big Speedway events. However, the scale of this place makes security problematic."

The Fire Chief added, "We pre-position several fire & rescue crews here on the grounds to respond to any emergency, but once we get to Speedway Boulevard, it's a real chore to get to our trauma centers. If we did have a major incident, response time would be a real problem."

As the Speedway manager escorted them outside, the mayor put his hand on the small of Sheryl's back as he led her though the doorway. She thought how nice it would be to lay into this guy one of these days. The manager brought them to the fanciest golf cart-looking vehicle she'd ever seen. When she got in, naturally Milton Fryer sat next to her. She thought how easy it would be to shoot him with the 9mm Beretta in her purse.

As they drove along the back of the grandstands, Jeff Bowden from Homeland Security asked, "What kind of construction is this?"

"Steel, concrete and aluminum, anything made of wood is long gone," replied the manager. "It's really quite safe from fire."

"That's really a necessity here because egress is limited. Unlike a football or other stadium, the fans can't run onto the field in an emergency," said the Fire Chief as the Speedway manager turned the cart into one of the pedestrian tunnels used to allow people into the stands. He went on, "You see, that's a fourteen foot fence that separates the fans from the track itself. It's there more to protect the spectators from flying debris than keeping people off the track, but it would act that way, nonetheless, in an emergency."

6

THE GROUP TOURED the remainder of the Speedway for the next hour and then left separately after
arranging tentatively to meet again in about six months.
That meeting would be for the International Airport
that was practically next door to the Speedway. Sheryl
thought as she began driving back to Jacksonville that
there could be some vulnerability here. The term *The
Great American Race* assigned to the Daytona 500 event
could draw the attention of some bad guys looking for
an iconic American target. A worse case scenario could
be a hijacked airliner, quickly diverted into the grandstands on final approach. There would be no defense
against it. Tomorrow, she would call and discuss this
with her boss at the Jacksonville field office. She would
probably recommend that the FAA suspend flights and
not allow any aircraft landings during major events at
the Speedway. She figured that the suggestion had no
chance of being accepted, but at least she could cover

her ass if something did happen. According to the mayor, the networks broadcast the race to over 130 countries, where millions of people watched it live. It would be a career killer for someone who ignored the threat and something happened. As remote as the possibility was, it was still worth going on the record as being the person who warned the officials of the possible danger. After all, that was her job.

She looked at the clock on the dash and figured with the traffic and all, she might as well go home instead of the office. She was still wet from perspiration after driving around in that golf cart in the hot afternoon sun. Her clothes felt even tighter than they had that morning, and what she needed was a nice shower.

As she pulled up to her building, she noticed his car in the parking lot. When she entered her condo he was lying on her bed wearing nothing but the fancy pair of expensive boxers that she had bought him. They didn't even bother to say hello to each other as she went right into her bathroom to undress and take a shower. As the water cascaded over her, she thought what a strange relationship they had. They didn't even like each other that much. She suspected that he might even lay awake nights thinking of subtle ways to insult her. The other night he had actually pinched a roll of her belly fat. They had been together for nearly four years now, and she figured their emotional attachment was akin to how two porn actors felt about each other during the act. She had no delusions that for him, it was anything more than sex and rough sex at that. She would occasionally come away with bruises, but she didn't care. She used to be concerned that some day people would find out about their relationship because they had worked together. They went to great pains making sure others didn't know. When traveling for the job, they would stay in adjoining rooms so that no one would see them coming and going. However, since his retirement a month ago, it wasn't really a problem—and if someone did find out, she didn't care, especially his ex-partner Beth who was totally clueless to what they were doing.

When they were finished, he got up, dressed and didn't even bother to say good-bye. This didn't bother Sheryl. At least he didn't leave a twenty-dollar bill on her dresser. He probably hadn't thought of that yet. Sheryl thought how different he was from her ex-husband with whom she hadn't spoken in ten years. Her ex' did pretty much what she asked, and when he wouldn't, she would always find a way to make it happen. She recalled her biggest triumph. The two were high school sweethearts and very popular. He had wanted to go to Annapolis. It had always been his dream to be a Naval Aviator.

At first, this sounded very romantic to Sheryl, but the notion lost its charm once she realized that she would be a Navy wife for ten or twelve years after his graduation. She had goals too. Sheryl wanted a law degree. Without the extra commitment the Navy added because of pilot training, her studies would be finished within a couple of years of his discharge. This would have been okay with her. However, four additional years of being a Navy wife with her career on hold was unacceptable. So for her ex-husband's first two years at the Naval

Academy she frequently told him how dangerous she thought flying was and that maybe he should reconsider. He didn't agree, so she switched to a more subtle tactic. She timed it so that she was never available when he called just before his exams. She also made subtle hints about her activities that made him question her fidelity. This tactic had the desired effect. In his last two years at the Academy, he did poorly and finished near the bottom of his class. He was passed-over when he applied for flight training. Sheryl found it somewhat amusing that the Navy decided to assign her poor performing student of a husband into Naval Intelligence. Sheryl and he did get married, but she divorced him about three years later. She never got around to changing back to her maiden name and supposed it was too late in her career to do it now.

Sheryl looked at the clock. It was early, and she decided go out and have a few glasses of wine. She was doing that a lot lately.

7

IT WAS FRIDAY AFTERNOON and Mark had been with the unit for five days, now. Beth had been right. Mark did ask a lot of questions, most of them valid, however. Mark seemed to be a nice person. He would probably work out well as her partner, she thought. However, he did have one habit that would have annoyed her a few years ago, and that was Mark, like many other men, didn't feel the need to look at her when he spoke. To Beth this seemed unique among the male gender. Women usually made eye contact when they conversed. When there was a meeting in a conference room, men sitting side-by-side would make no attempt to look at the person they were addressing. Women would generally lean over and try to make eye contact. She remembered a little spat she had with her late husband right after they moved into her present home. Her husband was watching the football game on TV and she couldn't seem to get his attention. Beth wanted to know what he wanted to do for dinner, and he being a rabid football fan didn't like the interruptions and said, "You've asked me that three times, already."

Beth answered crossly, "If you look at me when I talk to you, I'll know you're listening." From then on her husband used to tease her. When a game was on, and she asked him a question, he would do a perfect military right-face and give her an answer like he was speaking to a drill sergeant in boot camp.

Beth said to Mark, "How was your first week? Do you like this better than your old job chasing Wall Street crooks?"

"Yeah, I think this is a good career move. The one thing I did like about the old job though, you got out of the office more frequently to do interviews. It doesn't seem to be the case, here."

Beth would agree, especially now, with the new system. "Did you contact the other agents about that membership list from that mosque in Toronto?"

"I sent them an e-mail on Tuesday. They called while you were at lunch today. I planned to talk to you about it. It seems there is some activity. They're watching a number of people who apparently have some ties to Hezbollah and Iranian intelligence. They said it's a real hornet's nest. Apparently the Imam preaches what they described as propaganda and hate against America, the UK and Israel."

"Did they suggest anything?" Beth asked.

"One of the agents told me that he would assign at least a threat level five classification to anyone who belongs to that mosque."

"What do you think?"

"I don't know. I believe you told me the other day that anyone five and above has his or her calls intercepted by the NSA."

"That's right. It also means that you'll see a lot more activity, and the subject will show up more frequently in our queues. We'd want to think about it. That's a lot more data to sift through. I'll mull it over this weekend. By the way, do you feel you'll be able to comfortably access the system from home? Have you tried it yet? I have the duty on Sunday and you have it on Saturday. You understand, right?" Beth asked.

"Everything is all set, I can handle it."

"Good."

Mark wanted to leave it a little bit light-hearted for the weekend, so he asked Beth, "I have a question for you. I noticed that we have some Muslim women we're watching."

Beth said, "There are women bad guys, also."

"Well, if the men get 72 virgins when they're martyred, what do the women get when they go to Paradise?"

If Mark expected a smile or chuckle out of Beth, he didn't get it.

"Mark, that's the kind of thing that gets us in trouble. I know you're trying to be glib, but our lack of understanding about the Muslim culture sometimes keeps us from connecting the dots. Unlike your old unit where motivation isn't really a factor—what's that quote you hear all the time by Willie Sutton? . . . 'I rob banks because that's where the money is'. Things are different here. We have to understand the culture of our adversaries."

Mark didn't appreciate Beth's rebuke.

She went on. "Listen, Mark, the issue with the 72 virgins is a good example of our lack of understanding. I'm sorry, I don't mean to be so forceful, but this is the kind of thing that gets people killed," Beth said thinking about her late husband. "Let me explain about the virgins, and then I think you'll see my point. In some areas of the Middle East and North Africa, the number 72 has a meaning larger than the number itself. If a mother said to her child, 'If I told you once, I told you a thousand times not to do that', do you think the mother actually told the child a thousand times?"

"No, of course not," Mark answered, not liking being lectured by Beth.

"What is she actually saying?"

"She's telling the child that she's said the same thing over and over."

"The *seventy-two* to them is the *thousand* to us," said Beth. "The number seventy-two means abundance."

"The same thing goes with the word virgin. It's not just a girl who hasn't had sex, it's more of an idea of their perfect female: chaste, modest and untouched. She would be diaphanous in her purity." Beth continued, "Muslims believe they will reach paradise in one of two ways. Their religion expects a good Muslim to live a long life of piety where virtue and prayer are foremost.

Or, they can reach paradise in a shorter time through martyrdom."

"I think that as Americans it's hard for us to grasp the concept of intentionally depriving ourselves as well as our families of the good life. We want freedom to do what we wish, and we don't understand why all others in the world would not want to share in this notion. This is a real problem for many Muslims. Importing freedom also means importing temptation. As Western influence grows in their countries so does the temptation to succumb to these temptations and make it harder for them to reach Paradise. So they think, anyway."

"I never heard that before," said Mark.

"I don't think many of our political leaders have either," said Beth.

"So we may be at odds with ourselves?" returned Mark

"I think so," Beth said, looking at her watch. She wanted to end the conversation. She didn't want to be caught in the Friday night traffic trying to get out of Jacksonville.

"Mark, now let me answer your original question: What do Muslim women get in Paradise—they get free from the yokes placed upon them by men," Beth smiled as she got up and headed out.

8

BETH AWOKE EARLY even though it was Saturday and not a workday. She was alone because it was June, and her father spent the summers back in Maine at the family home. Her sister, her sister's husband and Beth's three nephews now inhabited it. Beth's father usually arrived in Jacksonville after Thanksgiving and would go back north in late May, just before the kid's school vacation. Her father would watch the boys in the summer months while her sister was at work as a nurse in the local hospital.

Beth's mother died of cancer the same year Beth's husband Jack was killed in Afghanistan. It had been over five years now and Beth and her father had settled down to a comfortable routine. She liked the company. Beth looked at the clock and decided to get up. She wanted to paddle the newly built kayak before delivering it to its new owner who had been waiting over a year. Beth was a master builder of these wooden craft since her high school days in Maine. She had learned the art from her father. He was well-known for restoring old wooded boats like those one would see on the upstate lakes of New York. After 15 years of lobstering the cold water and bad weather had taken a toll on his health so he began restoring old wooden boats, turning his hobby into a career.

Beth got dressed, went into the boathouse, and retrieved the new kayak. She hated to sell them. As she put the boat in the water she remembered how she felt the first time she let one go. As a teenager, she would help her father when his arthritis flared up. The drugs for that debilitating disease weren't as good then as they are today, she remembered. Under her father's scrutiny, she would make the cuts, do the sanding and whatever else was required. She also became adept in using the router and carving tools.

Beth didn't mind helping her father even though he was somewhat of a perfectionist. She eventually became so good at woodworking that her father stopped looking over her shoulder. In the summer of her junior year in high school, she decided to use the scrap mahogany and other expensive woods to fashion a beautiful wooden kayak for herself. It was complete with intricately carved inlays and polished fittings. It was nothing like the wooden kit boats that one could buy. One day while her father was delivering a restored 1941 Gar Wood cruiser, the customer spied the kayak suspended from the ceiling and asked if he could see it. He was so taken with the workmanship, he asked the selling price. Beth, who was walking through the door, heard the question and said it wasn't for sale. It was her personal boat. The customer offered her six thousand dollars, an offer she couldn't refuse and she sold it. Eventually, Beth made enough money building kayaks to put herself through college and pay for law school. Now, she built one boat a year, if that. Her job at the FBI and the remodeling work on her house took most of her time.

After paddling the boat upstream for about an hour, she headed back. As she approached her dock, she couldn't help feeling proud about the fine job she and her father had done on the house. From the water it looked fantastic. She would sometimes see other boaters slow down and look at her property. When she bought the old Key West style house it was in poor shape. It had even suffered through a flood in its 50 years of existence. Nevertheless, it was in a great location and had a forty-foot boat dock with a crumbling boathouse. It also had an outbuilding big enough for three cars.

Like most houses in Florida, it didn't have a basement, but sat on piers with a crawl space underneath. The first thing she did was sink fourteen-foot pilings closer to the water. This allowed riggers to move and then raise the house to FEMA standards. She was then able to purchase flood insurance and secure a home equity loan.

Over the next three years, she and her father rebuilt her entire home, both inside and out. They converted the porch that wrapped around three sides of the house to a giant deck. A set of stairs led first to a screened-in gazebo then down to the boathouse, which they had also rebuilt. On the other side, they did a similar thing.

There was an outdoor barbecue area on the first level, and then the stairs led to a pergola that stretched to Beth's workshop, which had previously been the garage.

They put white lattice work around the bottom of the house, hiding the piers, and installed garage doors that opened to allow her to park her car under the house. The effect of all this made the house look much larger than its 1,900 square feet of living space that included the loft that she used for a home office. The loft had windows on all four sides and gave Beth a great view of the river.

She had Sheryl over with the rest of the crew for a barbecue on the one Fourth of July. She remembered her ex-partner telling her how jealous it made Sheryl.

Thinking of Sheryl's *wish*, she decided to go check to see if Mark had worked the new items on the system. It was his duty day. Beth could get into TICS with the secure, encrypted connection she had in her home office. Mark had done the work as she expected. She would tell Sheryl on Monday that her wish had come true, and Mark was up to speed.

9

IT WAS FRIDAY, the weekly day of gathering for the Danesh and Naderi brothers at the Markaz al Islami Mosque. Since it was a nice summer day in Ontario the men rode their motorcycles to the short early afternoon service that all Muslim males are required to attend. Markaz al Islami was a common name for a mosque. It translated roughly in English to Islamic Center. The mosque had the familiar architecture of a dome with minaret where the *muazzin* would call the faithful to prayer five times a day. The Markaz al Islami Mosque also housed a community center for weddings, funerals and meetings as well as a number of classrooms for weekend school for young Muslim boys and girls. This was similar to Sunday school for Christians and Hebrew school for Jews. Children and young adults would gather at this weekend school to socialize with other Muslims and learn more about their faith. This is where Nouri and Sami had first met the Danesh brothers. It was 15 years ago when they were all children.

After the short service ended most people would go back to their jobs. However, the four young men stayed to talk with Kasra Khatani, who had been their teacher for the last ten years of their weekend schooling. They liked Kasra because he was soft-spoken and had many stories about the struggle. Unknown to them, and most of the mosque's membership, Kasra Khatani, not his real name, was one of the original members of Hezbollah who had fled Lebanon at a time when that organization was out of favor. He also had strong ties to Iran.

As a young man he was trained in terrorist tactics in the Beqaa Valley of Lebanon alongside a man who later became head of the Revolutionary Guards in Iran. The two men had remained friends ever since. They both shared the common vision of Jihad against the West. Kasra Khatani was involved in many terrorist acts before coming to Canada, including the 1983 bombing of the United States Marine barracks in Beirut that killed 241 American servicemen.

When he first landed in his new country, he made his home in Montreal for a time. That's where he began his career as a teacher in a local mosque. Unfortunately, he wasn't as adept as he was now at the fine art of recruiting young men for Jihad, and the mosque's elders asked him to leave.

This was the first time Sami had seen Kasra since returning to Canada for the summer. The two greeted each other warmly. "How do you like your schooling in America?" Kasra asked in his thick Middle East accent.

"It's not that great," answered Sami.

"They do not like Muslims there, no?"

"There's been a lot of trouble on our campus. The FBI has interviewed me twice. I made the mistake the first time of telling them my family was originally from Iran. That led to another couple hours of interrogation."

"Nouri, you went to the same university?"

"Yeah, but I never got interviewed by any agents."

About then, Nouri saw his father, who had also been at the service, heading their way.

"Nouri, you going back to work anytime today?" his father asked.

Nouri found it rather strange. His father hardly ever checked up on him or commented on his work habits. "I'm headed back now."

"Sami, your mother needs some help at home."

"OK, I'll head back with Nouri."

Nouri and Sami left the Danesh brothers talking to Kasra Khatani. He would see his friends later.

As he recklessly rode his powerful motorcycle, he thought about how much he liked and respected Kasra Khatani. He wished his father was more like him. Nouri remembered that before his grandfather became sick, he had showed the same kind of passion. Only, his grandfather's style was much different from Khatani's. Nouri and his brother Sami would love to get their grandfather going on the Israelis or the Americans. Nouri's father always tried to discouraged them from this, but the boys would do it every chance they got. Nouri probably didn't realize it, but subconsciously he was picking up his grandfather's attitudes. Later Kasra would reinforce these attitudes. He would frequently tell them "Islam's main enemy is the United States, who used Israel as a pointed spear to inflict sufferings on the Muslim people." He also quoted his former mentor, the Ayatollah Khomeini regularly, and his favorite quotation was, "America is the main reason for all our catastrophes and the source of all malice. By fighting it we are exercising our legitimate right to defend our Islam and the dignity of our nation."

As the boys were growing up Kasra Khatani had shared countless examples of how this was true. Most of this was hyperbole or outright lies. Of course, none of Khatani's remarks were known to Nouri's parents. He had urged his young followers to be tight-lipped about their talks.

A car quickly changing lanes knocked Nouri out of his reverie. He was racing back and forth with his brother weaving in and out of the rush hour traffic when it happened. "Jesus Christ" said Nouri and then flipped the guy off. Nouri would never take his own God's name in vain, but the Christian God was good for this purpose, he thought.

10

IF NOURI DIDN'T THINK his father knew about his work habits, he was mistaken. Ali Naderi was watching him more closely than he could ever have imagined. Ali was concerned. His son was spending more and more time at the Mosque with his friends the Danesh brothers. There were rumors that their father was connected with the Iranian Revolutionary Guards. He was also concerned that the three young men were spending much of this time at the Mosque, not in prayer, but in the company of Kasra Khatani.

Certainly, Ali Naderi had no love for the United States, but Khatani's views went well over the top. The only person he had ever met who hated the United States more was his own father, who was exiled from Iran when the CIA put the Shah in power. Lately Nouri seemed to be obsessed with America. When he joined the family for dinner, his conversations would always gravitate to an anti-American diatribe. Nouri sounded more and more like his grandfather every day. Ali was sure much of this acrimony was the result of Nouri and his friends hanging around Kasra Khatani and listening to his lunatic ideas. Ali thought it didn't take much nowadays to come to the attention of the authorities. So Ali had taken some steps himself to make sure this didn't happen.

Ali Naderi, before taking over his father's company, had been a partner in a small computer security firm. Ali had majored in computer science, as they called it in those days, from McGill University. He was one of the early adopters of personal computer technology and bought his first one, an Apple II-c, in 1980. Since then, he always had to have the latest and greatest system on the market. This translated to three or four new note-book computers a year, something Nouri and his brother Sami had benefited from. It was his custom to give the old one to one of his sons. The boys appreciated this practice, and their friends envied them. Ali was also monitoring his old profession. While he liked being wealthy and running the family company, computers were his passion, so he kept up with what was happening in the industry. This was especially true in computer security matters. So it was no problem at all for him to make a few modifications to the notebook computer he recently gave Nouri.

Ali took advantage of the fact that most modern personal computers used an operating system that would allow multiple people to use the same computer in privacy. So for example, a parent who had financial information on the computer didn't have to give access to their children. Each person had their own set of files and they were kept in an "account" as the industry referred to it. Usually, the main user would act as the "administrator", creating these accounts for others and choosing certain options. However, since there were times when a person did want to give access to someone else, the user could designate these files as shared files. They could also decide who on their computer could see these files on a home network, or for that matter, open them up to the entire Internet community. This was a handy feature for young people wanting to share music with their peers.

Since Ali had owned the computer initially, he usually kept himself as administrator and created another account for his son who would receive the computer. He would then transfer his files to his new notebook computer before erasing them.

Ali was troubled at the direction both his son's were heading. Sami was usually the level headed one, but he also was spending time with Kasra Khatani when he was home from school and had lately been enthusiastically joining Nouri with his tirades. Keeping this in mind, Ali had decided to find out what his sons were doing. For these reasons, Ali didn't give a second thought to invading their privacy. He had already put a key-logger in Nouri's notebook that would record every keystroke and mouse click Nouri made. He also installed a program that would copy each of his son's files. Ali set the program options to hide the copied files in his "account" and not show up anywhere on Nouri's directory structure. This account would be open to Ali anytime Nouri was on the Internet.

The other thing the program would do is copy the web-browser Index file. Most people who wanted to hide their Internet surfing activity knew enough to e-rase the browsers history file. However, an internal operating system file for speeding Internet navigation was always active and kept a record of web-browsing activity. Ali knew that was how many people were caught web surfing on company time. It was easy for the company's IT department to trace web-browsing using the Index File even after the person erased their history.

Ali also subscribed to a free web service that would download a program that would work quietly in the background to back-up all of his son's files to an off-site storage facility. It was all automatic and invisible unless you knew it was there.

All this enabled Ali to monitor Nouri's computer activity anytime he wished. However, it would have been more shocking for Nouri and his friends if they had known what else Nouri's father had done. Since the notebook computer was a top-of-the-line model, it was equipped with a built-in webcam and microphone. Ali had configured it always to be on, no matter what setting Nouri chose. His father could listen and watch anytime he wished from anywhere. Ali was doing a lot of this lately, and he didn't like what he was hearing in the old building. He noticed the young men were hav-ing frequent conversations about blowing things up. He might have dismissed these conversations had he not found that Nouri was actually recording these scenarios on his computer despite his friends' admonishments. It never ceased to surprise him about the lack of common sense and good judgment his son showed from time-to-time. It sometimes amazed him that Nouri was able to graduate college with an engineering degree, although it did take him five and a half years to do it.

11

THE NATIONAL SECURITY AGENCY'S job was to listen, analyze and report. Since the proliferation of the Internet, the term listening was expanded to include monitoring e-mail and website activity. It was on this expanded role that Nathan Niblock was preparing to brief his new boss.

Nathan was surprised to see his new director, retired Rear Admiral Payton Stiles, approaching him without an entourage. His old boss never seemed to travel the building alone. Since they had never met, he walked up and introduced himself. They shook hands and then the admiral looked down at Nathan's academy ring and asked, "What class?"

"95, Sir."

"I taught at Annapolis from 1998 to 2001, then moved on to the War College in Newport," said the admiral.

Nathan was happy his new boss noticed the ring. He planned to get the fact that he was a Naval Academy graduate in the conversation somehow. Nathan knew Academy graduates, after leaving the military, always tended to help each other, particularly inside the Beltway. It was a powerful network.

Nathan Niblock joined the NSA after his service in the Navy was completed. An alphabet soup of intelligence gathering agencies including the CIA, DIA, NSA, and many others whose names or initials were not common knowledge, had approached him. He chose the NSA because after moving around in the Navy for ten years, he wanted to put down some roots. Most NSA facilities were located in the Washington, DC area and for the most part, they didn't have agents on the ground in undercover roles.

Nathan had worked his way up to an assistant director in the software development unit. His responsibilities also included website development and monitoring.

"How many people do you have in your section, Nathan?"

"I have about two hundred and ninety in this building and another 55 in covert roles."

"That's quite a few people just to monitor e-mail and websites."

"Admiral, it would seem so." When Nathan first joined the area, he was surprised to learn that the NSA hosted 1,300 websites, many masquerading as discussion forums sympathetic to almost every lunatic group imaginable. He found it amazing what some people would share with each other on the Internet when they thought themselves anonymous. There were 230 websites dealing with radical Muslin activities alone, all developed by the NSA. Nathan explained this to his new Director.

"We are also one of the largest providers of software in the world, second only to Microsoft—only the public doesn't know it. I think you'd agree, Admiral, that it would be a real surprise for most people to learn that 95 percent of all free software for the detection and removal of viruses, spy-ware, root-kits, and key-loggers comes from us."

"Is that true?" said the Admiral, obviously surprised."

"Chances are good that if you download any free programs of this type, our software team developed it. This is also true for encryption. We have server farms dedicated for off-site storage, too."

"What do you mean by that?"

"We offer a free service so individuals and businesses can protect their data and recover it, in case of disaster."

"That's pretty impressive."

"Yes, sir. I think so."

"You said you have fifty people working covertly?"

"Fifty-five, sir."

"What do they do?"

"We have them embedded in the commercial software houses. Their job is to insert a piece of code in a computer program from time-to-time in major computer vendors' software."

"So, it sounds like if you use the Internet, chances are good that NSA is somewhere inside your computer?"

"That's correct, Admiral."

"How are we using the information?"

"We usually get an automated monitoring request from the FBI or CIA. They're both on a new system we developed here called TICS, Threat Identification and Classification System."

"How exactly does that work?"

"As you know, since the passage of the Patriot Act, sharing classified information among America's intelligence agencies has become much easier. It became so easy that our people were drowning in the data. So our section developed a system to collect the various pieces of intelligence data from many different sources, organize it and then display it remotely for the requester. It's used primarily by the FBI."

"At what cost?"

"You'll love this. One of the unintended but positive consequences of having 1,300 websites operating is the amount of advertising revenue we're generating. It's only September and we've surpassed fifty million dollars already. We developed TICS using last year's revenue. This year we've used most of the funds to deploy a database of voiceprints we gather from Interpol, Mossad and other foreign intelligence agencies. We're now in the process of integrating this function into the FBI and CIA's identification system, which should be ready by December."

"Too bad the tax payer will never know how well we're using their money," the Admiral said with a chuckle.

"Yeah, too bad."

"I'm sure you've looked into the legalities of all this data collection."

"There was a finding by the legal staff that it's okay to collect it as long as we don't look at it without a FISA warrant. We leave warrant requests with the FBI or CIA. When they ask for the information, we give it to them. We don't look at it ourselves."

"I'll have to look into that. By the way, where did you get your people?"

"Some are recruited, which is hard because of the competition from the private sector. As you can see, the working conditions are not exactly plush. We don't have people playing touch football in the corridors, and there are no 'bring your dog to work' days here."

"So what do you do?"

"When we need people we go trawling. We set up an attractive nuisance for hackers, usually the Department of Defense computers. When they break-in, if they're in the United States, we have the FBI scoop them up. If they can be of use to us we offer them a deal, a free vacation to Guantánamo Bay or a job with us."

"Are you serious?"

"Yes sir."

"I suppose we pay them."

"Oh yes. They're well paid, and we also allow them to continue some of their mischief."

"How's that?"

"Once a month as a reward for reaching the department goals they're allowed a major hack somewhere. Lately the 'denial of service attack is popular' primarily on the music industry. Most of these guys are mad because they can't download free music anymore."

"I've never heard of that. You say denial of service attack?"

"You've probably heard of computer hackers intentionally crashing a company's website?"

"Oh yeah."

"That's a denial of service attack."

"And you let them do this for entertainment?" The Admiral looked pensive.

"That's what they think. But every time they do it we're learning more about how to keep people from doing it to government computers, as well as possibly using this technique as a cyber weapon."

"Well, that's very smart."

"Thank you, Admiral."

"Thanks for the tour. When I get home tonight, I'm purging my computer," the admiral said, with a smile.

"Probably won't do any good, sir."

12

IT WAS THE THIRD FRIDAY in November, the
holy month of Ramadan, and Nouri was hungry. He
wondered if Sami, who was back in Florida, was ob-
serving the dawn-to-dusk fast. Nouri was listening to
the Imam giving his Friday afternoon sermon and getting about every third word. He thought it must be fiery
because of the reaction of the men in the main prayer
hall. His Arabic wasn't that good. His grandparents had
spoken Farsi at home, so he wasn't conversant in the
other language except for the Koran. He, like other de-
vout Muslims, had memorized most of the passages in
Arabic although not hearing the fluid, melodious nature
of the verses. He watched as the Imam stood red-faced
shouting something about America and Israel. Nouri
would ask Kasra Khatani what the Imam had said from
the pulpit, later. Kasra had invited him to dinner along
with Farid and Reza. They would be going to the
Moroccan restaurant they all liked.

When Nouri arrived at the restaurant everyone was already there. Besides Farid and Reza, there were two others along with Kasra Khatani. Nouri knew them but not well. They were a few years younger than even Reza, and this was the first time he had dined with them. They young men greeted Nouri with the formal, *Assalamu Alaykum*, peace be upon you. Nouri replied with the traditional answer when addressed this way, *wa alaikumus salam*, and peace be upon you.

Nouri knew this restaurant had great food. It was in the traditional style. Seating was close to the floor on either lounges or large pillows. There were nice tapestries adorning the walls and of course, Nouri's favorite was the belly dancer who was performing on the other side of the room. He arranged himself across from Kasra between Farid and Reza. It was always a good thing to separate the two. They settled themselves just as the server arrived with a basin and scented towels so the men could wash their hands. It was the custom to eat without utensils from communal pots and dishes. As usual Kasra did the ordering. He knew everyone was hungry from the day's fast, so he didn't hold back. They started with a nice Moroccan style salad then had *B'stilla*, which is a boneless chicken pastry, followed by chicken with lemon and finally Nouri's favorite, *Lham Mrhosia* or lamb with honey. Kasra also ordered a delicious vegetable couscous.

After dinner while the young men were having their mint tea, Kasra Khatani started to tell them about what he'd heard. Nobody ever questioned him about where he heard these things. That was the first thing you learned when you were accepted into Kasra's inner circle. He started the conversation by asking them if they were familiar with a place called Diego Garcia.

Reza, always trying to prove he wasn't stupid, took what he thought was a reasonable shot at the answer. "It's in South America, isn't it?"

Kasra smiled. "Not exactly, it's actually in the Indian Ocean."

"You are so stupid," said Farid.

"Did you know where it was?"

Kasra held up his hand to stop the exchange between the two brothers and said, "Diego Garcia is in the Indian Ocean about 4,000 miles from Tehran, which is much closer to Iran than United States. It's owned by the British, but the Americans use it as a secret military base."

Nouri said, "I've never heard of it."

"That is the Idea," said Kasra Khatani. "The Americans had the British exile all the islanders from this place. There is no way to get there except by military ship or plane. There is no reason why anyone would want to go there."

All Kasra's stories had enough truth in them to be believable if someone tried to check the facts. There was indeed a place called Diego Garcia, part of the Chagos Archipelago in the middle of the Indian Ocean about a thousand miles south of Sri Lanka's southern coast. The British asked the islanders to leave their coconut plantations in 1973, and since then the United States and the United Kingdom use the 37 mile long island covered in lush tropical vegetation as a military base. The United

States Navy uses the large lagoon as a safe harbor for their ships.

Kasra Khatani went on with his story, which contained some truth along with some wild assertions he thought might get the young men wound up. "The Americans have started moving their B2 Stealth Bombers to Diego Garcia preparing for an attack on Iran. They are also massing other military equipment there." Kasra didn't see his words having much affect, so he decided to relate a story that was so outlandish that even the gullible Reza might not accept it.

"This is bad enough that the Americans will attack Iran but not as bad as what I'm about to tell you." Kasra had their attention, maybe it might work he thought. "During the Iraq occupation by the Americans, a number of brave Iranian Revolutionary Guard volunteers crossed the border to help our Shiite Brothers."

Nouri and the others at the table had heard rumors and speculation about it but not many specifics. Nouri wondered were this was going. He heard Kasra saying, "Over five or six years, thousands crossed into Iran. Do you think it reasonable that no one was ever caught?

It didn't seem reasonable to Nouri and he said, "I've never heard that any Iranians were caught."

Kasra said, "There are over two hundred missing and not one of them is in the Guantánamo Bay concentration camp."

"Where are they?" Reza asked.

"They are in Diego Garcia. The Americans have a secret prison there." Kasra paused to let the point settle. "It is a place of torture and defilement, worse than anything you have heard about in Abu Ghraib. When the tormentors get the information they are seeking, they secretly execute the men." Kasra paused for effect.

One of the newcomers at the table said, "How do we know about the secret prison?" knowing that he had made a mistake right away by asking the question.

The other young men all looked at him. He had broken the rule, and they expected Kasra Khatani to banish him. Kasra thought this indiscretion might actually help him because it was a perfectly reasonable question, and since someone actually asked it aloud, he would give them an answer—this time.

"I do not know, but remember in addition to the men who interrogate and torture, there are interpreters. I am sure there are not that many intelligence people who speak Farsi. There are also translators to record what was being said for others to read. Our Iraqi friends also knew about the capture." He could see that they were surprised that he answered the question. He believed it was adding credibility to what he was telling them, so he continued.

"Nobody knows they are there. There are no organizations to check on their treatment. The Americans can do what they want to these men and never be held accountable. There is no angry press to denounce this treatment. In the end, they will all be killed because the Americans can never let them go."

Kasra Khatani could see that this was upsetting to the young men. There was silence at the table.

After they finished their mint tea, everyone said the traditional goodbye and left. Kasra thought, that went well. It always amazed him that people were so anxious to believe a lie.

13

THE YOUNG MEN were upset—mainly Farid—about the things Kasra Khatani had told them in the Moroccan restaurant that night. Farid seemed obsessed with the idea that Americans were torturing and executing Iranian prisoners. For the next two weeks, Farid used Nouri's computer, pouring over the Internet looking for any references to Diego Garcia that he could find. At first Nouri found this surprising. Usually when the brothers were over at his place they were arguing about whose turn it was on the game console, but Farid hardly touched the controller. Every time he did find something to back up Kasra Khatani's story, he would call Nouri over to look at what he found. There were references to secret prisons and discussion about the B2 stealth bombers. He saw that the Americans were indeed using the island as a forward supply base for possible strikes in the Arabian Peninsula. It appeared to them that everything Kasra Khatani told them was probably the truth.

Nouri remembered what his grandfather had told him about the American support of the shah and how the tyrant took reprisals out on many Iranians when he regained power. So it wasn't a very big leap for Nouri to believe that the Americans might be torturing and executing Iranian prisoners.

Farid, on the other hand, seemed totally convinced. Nouri thought he was always an angry person. There seemed to be in him a level of violence that simmered just below the surface. He usually directed the anger at his brother or the world in general, but now it was focused completely on the United States of America. Nouri could not remember either of the brothers doing anything important in their young lives. Commitment seemed to be not in their nature. So in Nouri's mind, Farid's fixation with the subject started becoming ominous. In the next week or so, his talk of targeting the United States became more than idle conversation for the young man. Nouri thought that Farid was now earnest in his quest to find an actual target in the United States. By now, Reza was caught up in the fervor of his brother, and their conversations took on a menacing tone.

Nouri couldn't exactly remember the point when he joined the mission, but by the time Sami returned home after the fall semester, Nouri was totally committed.

As soon as Farid saw Sami, he started in about what Kasra Khatani had told them and what he wanted to do about it. Sami, like his brother Nouri, had never seen

Farid so passionate about anything. Sami listened to Farid's diatribe at first with some amusement, but then something happened. Sami wasn't a happy person lately. His life was not going well. If he hadn't had one more semester left, he would have left USF for a Canadian school. The FBI had talked to him again, and it seemed that other students, knowing he was Muslim, were avoiding him. The roommates with whom he had shared an apartment since his sophomore year had moved out. When he questioned them about why, they used the archaic phase—he was *cramping their style*. He suspected that was a euphemism for they didn't want to live with a Muslim any longer. The other thing that bothered him was that he hadn't had a date in the last two years. It seemed that nobody wanted anything to do with him, and it made him bitter. So when Farid started in about what he wanted to do, Sami didn't say no.

Farid was back on the computer and the others were sitting around the table in the building's office area. "Let's figure out how to blow up these people," Farid said.

"Be realistic, we can talk about it all we want, but when it comes down to it, we're not going to kill anybody," said Nouri.

Sami added, "Farid, it would be just as good to show these people that we can kill them. Every time there's an incident, the American's overreact. Do you remember the idiot who tried to set a bomb off in his shoe? Now they make you take your shoes off to go through security at the airport. If we do something to make them afraid, I think it would be good enough. We let them know we can hit them anytime we want. They'll get scared and force their government to stop the crap."

"There's no way we're smuggling explosives into the United States even if we could get them," said his brother.

"Shut up, Reza," said Farid. "Nouri, you can make the explosives, right?"

"If I had access to the materials—but that could be risky, too," Nouri answered.

"What did McVey use in Oklahoma City," asked Farid.

"It was mostly diesel fuel and ammonium nitrate from fertilizer mixed in barrels. It was easy for them because supposedly McVey's partner had access to a farm. Four Iranian guys from Canada might attract a little attention pulling up to a supply store with a dump truck, aye?" replied Nouri.

"What do you suggest?" asked Farid.

"Well, if we were going to do it and not actually hurt anybody I'd want to make a big bang. We all work for the same company, except Sami, right? At least when you guys are working."

"Screw you."

"When one of the tankers needs welding, what's the first thing you do?" Nouri asked.

"It depends," said Reza. "If the tank is more than a quarter full, we fill it up right to the top. And if its less than a quarter full, we drain it, fill it with nitrogen and then wash it out," continued Reza.

"You know I never got that," said Farid. "How you could weld on a tanker full of gasoline."

Nouri answered, "You need oxygen for combustion. I remember seeing my grandfather throw a lit match in a bucket of diesel fuel and the match going out. You have to mix most fuels with oxygen to ignite. When the tank is full to the top there's no air. The most dangerous thing in the tanker yard is an empty truck because of fumes. That's why we fill them with nitrogen before trying to clean them."

"So what's your idea?"

"I say we use some sort of thermo-baric device."

"I guess you did learn something in those six years you were in college—big words."

"It wasn't six years. The military calls them FAEs or fuel/air explosives," said Nouri

"Where do we buy one of those?" asked Reza.

"At any hardware store—what an idiot," said Farid.

"We don't buy it, Reza. We make it," said Nouri. "That's the easy part. You can use anything, gasoline, diesel, avgas, racing fuel or any liquid that burns. Of course, the higher the octane rating the hotter it burns. But it doesn't make that much difference. The harder part is mixing in the air."

"That doesn't make any sense," said Farid

"Sure it does, you've seen those safety videos of fuel truck accidents, there's fire but no explosion. You have to mix oxygen with the fuel to get a big bang. Think about how the fuel injection system on your motorcycle works—the more oxygen the more power. Farid, that's what that thousand dollar nitrous system on your bike does. Nitrous Oxide mixes more oxygen with your fuel. If you can somehow get a cloud of fuel vapor and then ignite it, you'll get a huge explosion. Like I said, the military uses it against soft targets mainly, like people and vehicles. If somehow you could turn a full tanker truck into fuel vapor and then ignite it, the explosion could be equal to a small battlefield nuclear weapon. Let me show you something."

Nouri went to the YouTube website and found some videos he was looking for. "Take a look at this," he said.

The thirty second video clip showed a spectacular rocket explosion. "The fuel in this rocket was gasoline and liquid oxygen."

They watched ten or eleven more rocket explosions, and Farid was convinced this was the way to go. "So what do we do, steal a tanker truck in the States?"

"Yup, that's exactly what we do. I can figure a way to make it go bang," Nouri said.

"So does everybody agree to do this?" asked Farid with determination in his voice.

"Only if we don't try to kill anybody," replied Sami.

Nouri and Reza just nodded.

"So if we're not killing anybody, it's got to be someplace where a lot of people will see it."

"I agree," said Nouri. "Without an audience, it's just another tanker truck fire. We've talked about this before. I liked my Daytona idea."

"What Daytona idea?" asked Sami, who wasn't there at the time of the conversation.

"You went to the Daytona 500 last February, right?"

"Yeah, it was one of the only good times, I've had in Florida. There was a huge number of people there. It cost me thirty bucks to park across the street from the

Speedway because all the lots were filled by time I got there."

"Was the blimp there?"

"Actually, there were two of them."

"What do you think about setting off an explosion during the race?"

"It's a good possibility. Nouri, we're both familiar with the area and I'm only a couple of hours away in Tampa."

"Farid, what do you think?"

"I say we go for it."

"Okay then, let me think this through and work out some details," said Nouri.

"This is going to be good."

14

NOURI WAS CONVINCED he could make a bomb out of a fuel tanker truck with a little ingenuity. He hadn't used his chemical engineering degree since he graduated, but Nouri still remembered a good deal of what he had learned. He usually paid attention when the subject turned to petrochemicals because of the family business. It was a Monday afternoon so they would be able to get the supplies they needed. They already had plenty of fuel oil. Nouri knew that gasoline would be much too volatile for his experiments, but that would be the fuel of choice in the end.

The first stop they made was the local home store where they bought a charcoal grill, the kind with the dome cover. Since they were going to destroy it, they bought a knock-off instead of the brand name, which was much less expensive. While they were there, they also grabbed four lighters, the ones with the long tube used to light fireplaces or candles in the little red jars—

the type that keep you from burning your fingers. Next, the brothers headed for the chemical supply company that Sami had called earlier. When Nouri had told Sami that he wanted hydrogen peroxide, Sami said that their mother had bottles of the stuff in the house. She used to gargle with it to help her with her gum problems. Nouri laughed imagining how it felt to rinse your mouth with a 50 per cent solution of H_2O_2 instead of the medicinal three percent. He explained to his brother that in higher strength levels hydrogen peroxide helped oxidize the fuel to enhance combustion. Sami called around and wasn't able to find anything greater than forty percent. Nouri figured that would probably work. After all, wasn't that what experimentation was all about?

They were lucky because the chemical place also had the last thing they needed and that was liquid oxygen. Most people where familiar with it because of the U.S. space program. NASA referred to it as LOX. It was the white steam seen venting from the space shuttle when it was sitting on the launch pad. The most common use though, was supplying oxygen to people at home who needed it for breathing problems. They remembered that when their grandfather was sick, a truck used to deliver it. Sometimes Nouri or Sami would have to fill their grandfather's lightweight oxygen bottle from the 120 lb dewar, which looked like a fat thermos bottle. The dewar kept the liquid oxygen at minus 274° Fahrenheit and was stored outside because it wasn't easy to move around. There was a mechanical device that turned the liquid oxygen into a gas, so that their grandfather could use it to help him breath. They certainly didn't need 120 lbs. That was almost 34,000 liters of gas by Nouri's calculation. The smallest amount they could buy was thirty liters of the liquid, which was more than enough for what Nouri wanted to do.

The brothers then stopped by their home, and Nouri ran into the house to grab a few aluminum pie plates, a measuring cup and the longest soup ladle he could find. While he was there, he called Farid and Reza to come watch. They would be out of work in a half hour. It was already starting to get dark.

After they reached the old garage, Sami started assembling the charcoal grill. "Sami, don't be too fussy with that. We'll end up destroying it anyway."

"Yeah?"

"When you're through, drag it out back where no one can see us."

The day before Nouri had grabbed an old fire protection suit from one of the distribution terminals. He'd seen it many times but wondered who had ordered it. If there was a fire while they were filling gasoline trucks, he didn't know anybody foolish enough to stick around and fight it. They would get as far away, as fast as possible. The suit was shiny metallic-looking and consisted of a hood, jacket and bib pants. He put the thing on and when his brother saw him, he laughed so hard that he ended up rolling around in the snow that was in the back of the building. "You look like the Tin Man on the Wizard of Oz. Wait until Farid sees you," Sami said, still choking with laughter.

Nouri supposed he did look ridiculous, but Sami would understand when he started working with the

LOX. Nouri went back inside to get a table he needed and looked for some paper cups. When he returned the Danesh brothers were pulling up. Sami was right about Farid's reaction to Nouri's fire suit.

Nouri laid everything out neatly on the table. He put one of the aluminum plates inside the gas grill, measured exactly one ounce of fuel oil and poured it into the plate. He retrieved one of the lighters, pulled the little trigger and touched the flame to the fuel oil. Nothing happened. He'd seen his grandfather do this many times. He swished the fuel oil about and then held the flame one inch above the liquid and it flamed — nothing spectacular though. He put another pie plate over the burning liquid to smother the flame. Nouri then mixed one ounce of fuel oil with one ounce of hydrogen peroxide, swished it around and held the lighter an inch above the mixture. This time the flame was much higher and the young men could feel the heat in the cold air. While it was burning, Nouri had Sami fill the ladle with LOX from the container. "Stand back." Nouri said loudly. He poured the liquid oxygen on the flaming mixture spilling some on the area surrounding the pie plate. It blazed a good 10 feet in the air. It was so hot it started melting the aluminum, so Nouri closed the lid on the grill and something quite unexpected happened. It exploded.

Everyone had moved back far enough so no one but Nouri was hit by the burning liquid and metal pieces of the grill cover. Sami and the others could now appreciate the silly looking fire suit. Nouri had made his bomb.

The young men continued their experiments. Nouri wanted to see what would happen if they poured liquid oxygen into the fuel oil and hydrogen peroxide when it wasn't already lit. As he poured the oxygen into the liquid, it began to froth and bubble as the oxygen warmed. He put the lighter above the mixture and pulled the trigger. The lighter failed to light, but the spark was enough to ignite a huge flame. That gave Nouri an idea.

The young men continued to play with the fuel oil and liquid oxygen until they actually melted the charcoal grill. They left a small pile of scorched, twisted metal on a bare patch of ground. Sami hoped that his father wouldn't notice it if he decided to drop by. Even though it was in back, it would be noticeable from the office window. Sami went in the rear door of the garage and retrieved a snow shovel. When he came back out, Farid Danesh was laughing at his younger brother, Reza, who had picked up some of the hot metal and burned a hole right through his glove. Reza now had his hand in the snow. Sami started shoveling snow to cool off the metal, ignoring the immature behavior of Farid. When the others removed the debris, Sami spread some snow around the bare spots, wondering if the grass would grow back in the spring. When he finished, he surveyed his work and figured it looked all right. With all the footprints around the area and the forecast for snow, probably nobody would notice. As he thought about it though, they had been foolish. The front of the old building faced a busy street. They had waited until dark. Some observant passer-by could have noticed the black smoke coming from the rear of the building—luckily, nobody reported it.

Later on, Nouri would do another stupid thing by recording his experimentation in his laptop.

15

THEY WERE BACK IN THE CLUBHOUSE section of the old building getting warm. Everyone except for Sami was excited. Reza asked, "Nouri, how would we set the explosion off?"

Farid answered, "Reza, you climb up on the truck, open the manhole and hold the lighter over the fuel."

"Screw you"

Nouri said, "Reza, that's a good question. I was thinking about that myself. I may have an idea on that. Sami, remember when the lighter just sparked, and it lit the fuel anyway?"

"Yeah, that's how you light a butane torch or a gas grill. All you need is a spark."

Nouri was typing on his notebook computer and told the others to look. He pulled up a website selling stun guns, which was a misnomer because none of them actually looked like guns.

Reza said, "That says a million volts. I bet that would knock you on your ass, aye?"

Farid grabbed the mouse and clicked on another one. "Look, they have some disguised as cell phones."

Nouri said, "Sami, any one of these would give us a spark big enough to ignite the fuel and oxygen, particularly if the fuel was gasoline. Could you take one of these and build it so we could use it by remote control?"

"Sure," Sami said confidently. One more semester and he'd have his electrical engineering degree from USF.

"These all work the same way. You push a button or on this one here or you pull a trigger and it discharges a spark. You could remove the button circuitry and substitute a cell phone. I could wire it so when it rings or vibrates it would cause the stun gun to spark. The big cheap one here would work best. I could pick up a throwaway cell phone at a discount store. But where would you put it?"

"Farid just told us."

"I did?"

"When you told your brother to open the man hole on top of the tanker truck."

"You want Reza to hold the device above the man-hole?"

Reza said, "Now you guys know who the stupid one in the family really is. You're going to attach it under the lid, right."

"Sami, could you make it small enough to fit?" asked Nouri.

"Most of those manholes are twenty inches across, aren't they?"

Farid said, "Yeah, some are smaller. They're all twenties on our trucks." He and his brother were back working for Nouri's father, filling and cleaning the tankers.

Sami said, "No problem, nine or ten inches is all I need."

"What about mixing the fuel with the oxygen and all that stuff?" Reza asked.

Nouri thought for a minute. Let's figure we get our hands on a 9,000 gallon tanker, a 14,000 would be better. We grab the truck and move it somewhere where people won't see us. Two of us will climb up the ladder to the top and open the manhole. The others can pass up five or six gallons of hydrogen peroxide. We pour that in. We then attach Sami's contraption to the underside of the lid. Now, here's the hard part; we have to get a heavy LOX container to the top of the truck."

"What are we going to do with it once we get it up there," asked Farid.

"Open the valve on the oxygen and drop the tank through the manhole. It should fall to the bottom and bubble up the oxygen. If we block off the vents on the top of the truck with duct tape, in fifteen or so minutes the gas and oxygen will be under pressure or at least have some aeration."

"Farid, it works like the cylinders in a car or motorcycle. The gas and air are compressed by the piston and the spark plug ignites it," Sami added.

"We should cause one big-ass explosion," said Nouri.

"How do we get the truck?" asked Sami.

"I don't know. I haven't figured that part out yet," answered Nouri.

Farid smiled, "If you or your smart brother there ever did any real work in your dad's company then you'd know how to get the truck."

"Huh?"

"I'll bet it works the same way everywhere. The drivers get paid a lot more than we do filling the trucks. They're always under the gun to keep to the schedule. They have lots of stops. What stupid over here and I do, is fill the trucks and park them. We always have more trucks than drivers who call the foreman after their last stop to let us know he's bringing in an empty. The foreman tells one of us to start a truck and let it idle."

Sami asked, "Why do we do that?"

"Air brakes."

Nouri saw where this was heading right away. "Our trucks have air brakes. There has to be enough pressure built up in the compressor for the brakes to operate, usually about 120 psi. Until the pressure's built up, you're not going anywhere because the spring brakes won't release."

Nouri had driven the trucks many times but Sami hadn't. Their grandfather taught Nouri, but Sami was too young.

Farid said, "We snatch the truck when it's idling."

"Suppose someone catches us?" asked his brother.

"We get a few of these." Farid said while pointing to the stun guns, which looked like cell phones on the website. "If anybody bothers us, we zap em'." Farid smiled when he said that, probably still thinking of violence.

Nouri liked the idea. He thought Farid was probably right. It would make sense for someone in the fuel distribution business to operate this way. There were maybe twenty or so companies within a hundred mile radius of Daytona Beach. Surely, one of them would do it this way. He thought Sami could scout it out when he went back to Florida.

Reza asked, "How do we get down to Daytona Beach?"

"Either fly or drive," Nouri answered.

"I figured that," said Reza.

Farid said, "Nouri, go back a second. You said we have to get the liquid oxygen container to the top of the truck, right? How big is it? How much does it weigh?"

"The big supply companies usually have them in three sizes. The largest one won't fit through the manhole. The next size weighs 120 lbs and is 32 inches by 14 inches."

Sami, thinking Reza probably didn't know how to make the conversion to metric said, "That's about 55 kilos and 80 centimeters tall and 35 centimeters across."

Nouri continued, "We'll probably need two of them, which will give us about sixty liters of liquid oxygen."

Sami said, "I see a problem already."

"Where?"

"You can't fit two of those in a trunk of a regular car. You'll need a pick-up or full size SUV. By the way, if you did fly down to Florida, how were you planning to get around? Get a rental car? You'd be leaving a nice paper trail for the authorities to follow. You can't rent a car with cash either, it has to be on a credit card."

Nouri said, "Yeah, that's a problem. Unless we take the Suburban you use when you're home. We can drive it down and drive it back."

"What would be better is driving it down and leaving it for me in Florida. At the end of the semester I can use it to bring all my stuff back home. You guys can fly back."

They all agreed that way was probably the best way. They would fly out of Daytona Beach on the Sunday afternoon of the race after they blew up the truck. In fact, they could call the cell phone from the air terminal. They might even have a good view. Nouri said, "Okay, I'll make reservations for the three of us and put in on my credit card. There's no way around that, but we won't need a rental car, and we can stay at Sami's apartment since his roommates moved out. You guys can pay me back for the tickets when you have the money." Nouri knew he'd never see the money from either of the two brothers, primarily Farid.

"That's sounds good," said Farid, probably thinking the same thing.

Sami said, "Speaking of cash, big brother, where do I get the money for all the stuff I've got to buy?"

"Before you go back to Florida I'll give you a thousand. That should cover everything we need."

"What about the stun guns?"

"Sami, buy the one you need to make the detonator down in Florida. Use some of the cash. They'll have them at gun shops. I'll get the ones Farid likes so much online. You get the hydrogen peroxide and order the oxygen. We'll pick it up with the Suburban on Friday before the race when we get down there."

Reza asked, "Listen, will your father get pissed that all three of us miss work for a week?"

"Well, if we leave on a Tuesday and share the driving, we should be there on Friday. The plan is to fly back on Sunday. So I guess we're all out of work for four days. Yeah, my father won't be happy."

16

AFTER DISCUSSING a few more details, Farid and Reza wanted to try the new Flight Simulator that Nouri bought and installed on the game machine. Besides his notebook he had a computer he purchased and used just for games. Everything else he did on the notebook his father gave him. While the others were playing with the new Flight Simulator, he ordered the three cell phone looking stun guns. After that, he navigated through the travel sites to see if he could find some good ticket prices.

"Reza, order a pizza. I'll pay for it," said Nouri. Farid and Reza argued about the toppings as usual, and Nouri went back to his computer looking for a good airfare. About twenty minutes later, he was a little frustrated. One-way tickets from Daytona Beach to Toronto were expensive. Then Nouri had an idea. He made reservations for the three of them, leaving Daytona Beach International Airport at 4:20 P.M., using a small discount airline, and flying to Buffalo. They could then bus it back to Toronto. Nouri thought this would be perfect. They would have plenty of time to do what they needed to do and arrive home in Toronto before midnight. He could save $1,200 on the tickets. As he finished, the pizza arrived, so he took a break. While they were eating Sami asked, "Do you have any thoughts about where we put the truck when we get to the Speedway?"

"I picked up a map of Daytona Beach at the Autoclub. We can look at it after we're through here. You can also use Google Earth to see a satellite view of the area. It'll show us where all the buildings are. Reza, why don't you clean this mess up, so I can use the table for the map."

While Reza was cleaning up, Nouri found the satellite view he wanted. Then he accessed the Speedway's website, which helped him orient himself. The two best spots appeared to be at Turn 1 or Turn 2, as described on the Speedway's website. He wasn't sure, but the Turn 2 location might even be visible from the airport terminal. He grabbed the map and laid it on the table. He had the wrong side so he flipped it over. Apparently, Reza hadn't done such a good job cleaning up as the map now had a brownish red stain that looked like blood right over the Speedway. "Reza . . ." Nouri said.

"I was still working on it."

"Alright, come here guys. Look at this. Here are the two best spots. We park the truck on Williamson Blvd. at Turn 1 or Midway Blvd. at Turn 2. Most of the spectators are along here." Nouri showed them on the computer screen. "Sami, you can check it out when you go back to Florida."

"Both places are pretty close to the spectators on this end," Sami said, pointing to the Speedway's seating chart on the website.

"Can't be helped. There's a high bank right here at the turns, which should deflect most of the blast. I know we're not trying to hurt anybody, but we're blowing up a truck," replied Nouri.

"Maybe we should use a smaller truck," said Reza.

Farid said, "Little brother, you know what I'm going to do first when Nouri gets those stun guns . . ."

Reza had no doubt his brother meant what he said. He figured he better keep his month shut for the next few weeks.

"Come on. The Americans are torturing and killing Iranians, and you're worried about them," said Farid banging the table.

"Okay, settle down," said Nouri. "Sami, you're also scouting out the fuel depots for a couple of good possibilities. Is that junker you're driving around in Florida still working?"

"It'll be okay, but I don't think I want to try driving it back to Canada."

After they hashed out a few more details, they left Nouri alone. Not wanting to forget anything, he organized the information into a plan he put into his computer. Then he printed it out and later erased the file just to be safe. He didn't know that the file was both backed up on his machine and automatically sent to an offsite location operated by the NSA.

17

IT WAS SUNDAY IN EARLY JANUARY and bitter
cold in Toronto that morning. A blast of arctic air
had pushed the jet stream as far south as northern
Florida. It was minus fifteen degrees outside. Ali Naderi
thought to himself that it was a good day to stay home
and catch up on a few things. This he would do after he
finished reading the paper. It had been a few months
since Ali had downloaded Nouri's files from the back-
up site. He noticed that Nouri and Sami were acting a
little strange when Sami was home on holiday from his
studies. It probably was a good time to check up on his
sons. While he was reading the paper he would do the
download, which he figured would take a couple of
hours with his high-speed internet cable connection.

Ali had previously set-up a separate partition on his
hard drive where he could download the back-up files
without disturbing his data. He would then erase the
files after he reviewed them. This time the data transfer

took longer than he thought. It wasn't until after 3:00 P.M. that he heard the familiar ding that signified that the back-up was complete. By then, Ali was bored and looking for something to do. Dinner was four hours away.

Five hours later, after he told his wife he wasn't hungry, Ali sat at his big desk with his head in his hands. Ali actually said aloud, "I've raised a complete moron."

If Nouri was home, Ali would have killed him. What an imbecile I've raised, Ali thought. That damn Kasra Khatani must have something to do with this stupidity. Ali figured he better bring Aram Danesh in on this, too. He didn't like the man. He didn't trust him. He thought that he was a brute. Many times over the years Ali had seen Aram beat his two sons, but mainly Farid. He always felt sorry for the boys and when they were old enough, he gave them jobs in his company. Now the Danesh sons were also involved.

Ali figured that he and Aram Danesh should go together and confront Khatani. The elder Naderi didn't want Nouri to know he was spying on him until it was absolutely necessary, so he planned not to say anything to his son when he got home. That, he thought, will be hard.

Ali Naderi phoned Aram Danesh and explained everything. Aram, surprisingly, seemed upset and agreed that they should confront Khatani. Aram Danesh knew about Khatani's activities because of his frequent trips back to Iran. But Aram Danesh never thought that Khatani would involve his sons in anything like this. He expressed these thoughts to Ali. The men would talk to

Khatani tomorrow following the afternoon prayer. Ali printed out Nouri's detailed plan and went into the kitchen to find something to eat. All of sudden he was very hungry.

18

K ASRA KHATANI WAS WALKING out of the main prayer hall when he saw Ali Naderi and Aram Danesh walking toward him. They both had determined looks. Aram, who considered Kasra a friend said, "Kasra, we want to talk to you in private."

Khatani led them to one of the classrooms and Aram tried to sit at a student desk, which was much too small for his 275 lb bulk. Kasra almost laughed, but he figured he better not. These men seemed upset. Ali took out a folder and handed it over. When Khatani realized what it was, it floored him. "What's this?"

"I found that on Nouri's computer yesterday afternoon," said Ali Naderi.

Kasra didn't know what to make of it and didn't know what the men wanted from him, so he didn't say anything.

Ali went on, "I also found evidence that this thing is real and not just some fantasy. It appears our sons are planning on going through with this."

It took a lot to shock Kasra Khatani, but that's what he was now. Still somewhat puzzled he asked, "What do you want from me?" He had lapsed into Arabic.

Aram answered in the same language, "We want to know, what you know about this."

"Nothing."

Both Aram and Ali looked skeptical. Ali said, "Are you telling me that our sons came up with this on their own?"

"I don't know anything about it, but I'll ask around. People tell me many things."

"I bet they do," Ali said.

Khatani wanted to think. This getting out could jeopardize his covert activities. So he said, "Leave that with me." He was surprised when Ali handed the plan over. The men said their formal goodbyes and walked out.

Kasra sat down and started studying the plan. Now he knew why the men were skeptical. It was as good as anything he'd seen in his past. He also found it hard to believe the young men had come up with it. He thought it could even work.

That night, Kasra Khatani met with his Iranian contact, the man who was arranging his monthly five thousand dollar payment. He handed the plan over to him and explained the circumstances.

Exactly one week later, Kasra answered a knock on his door. He found his contact along with three other men standing there. Kasra ushered them in and offered a seat. His contact doesn't introduce them, and Kasra didn't ask their names. One of the men started to speak. "The Americans and their Israeli puppets will continue with their deceit and aggression. They have our brave suicide bombers killing their Muslim brothers and sisters. Only these diabolical Americans could figure ways to do this. They have pitted one Muslim against another, while they claim to be offering freedoms that nobody wants. When our martyrs do strike against them, their media allies don't even bother reporting it anymore. These Americans have become arrogant. They don't feel we can touch them on their homeland."

Kasra wondered where this was going. Another one of the men spoke, "We have studied the plan that you have brought us and it is sound. We will show the Americans that they are not safe from our reach and cannot go on killing our people with the help of the Israeli dogs. We congratulate you and your young men."

Kasra Khatani figured there had to be some misunderstanding. Did they actually want him to carry this out with the Naderi and Danesh brothers? Before he had a chance to ask, his contact smiled and said, "We will adopt this plan, but we will use our own men. Of course, we will make a few small changes. We will place the truck so that we can show the Americans that we can inflict much pain and suffering on them, also—and this man . . ." He pointed to the other man in the room. ". . . will see paradise for his brave efforts."

He went on, "This is what we want you to do."

After the four men left, he reflected on what he was told to do. He hadn't participated in anything like this for twenty years. True, he was still a member of Hezbollah, but his job was recruitment, raising money and giving information to the Iranians.

These men seemed to trust him and by their accents he figured that they were Lebanese. This probably meant Hezbollah. His organization had become much stronger in the Middle East lately and he figured it was a good time to reach out globally. The men were right. The Americans were arrogant, he thought. They will see. Kasra had some work to do first.

After thinking about how he would handle it, Kasra called and requested Aram and Ali meet with him the next afternoon at the mosque.

When the men showed up Kasra addressed both men, "You haven't spoken with your sons about that matter yet, have you?"

"No, we were waiting for you to get back to us," answered Ali.

"That is a good thing, because I have some news." Khatani said.

He went on, "I have made some discreet inquiries. I don't want to alarm you, but there is a slight possibility that your boys could be in some danger."

"What do you mean, some danger?" asked Ali.

"There are others who are involved in this plan, so we should take some precautions," answered Kasra. "Let me reassure you, your sons will never go through with this crazy scheme, but I need some time to handle the others who may not want to be stopped."

"What do you want us to do?" asked Ali.

"Do not mention we are on to them. Here is what I want you do."

Kasra Khatani thought the men seemed satisfied with his solution. It seemed easy enough and might work.

19

MARK SIENE HAD BEEN IN HIS NEW JOB for seven months now, and he wondered if he had made a mistake taking the position. He was finding it dull; there wasn't that much going on. When he first joined the unit, back in June, the threat management system was only a few months old. They were still adding new contacts. Beth and Mark were busy analyzing all the data, but by the end of the summer, the flood of new information had all but dried up. When they did get a hit, they worked the subject to death. Mark heard other agents in the unit were doing the same thing. It was hard for them to stay busy, so the teams started assigning higher and higher threat level classifications to those individuals residing in their queues just to generate more activity. This worked for a while, but now it was mid-January, and they were back looking for stuff to do. It was rumored that the FBI planned to reassign many of the counter terrorism agents, but so far there was no official word of that happening. Mark and Beth rarely had the opportunity to leave the field office, and it was getting monotonous. Mark remembered hearing from a couple of agents who stopped by from Tampa, that they were spending a lot of time at the University of South Florida interviewing foreign students.

Mark figured that of the now 1,200 people assigned to them only two were even remotely interesting—the Naderi brothers, Nouri and Sami. Beth had changed Nouri's classification to a seven, which was total overkill. They were getting transcripts of all his cell phone calls, text messages as well as listings of his web-browsing. Mark knew that Beth was currently going through Nouri Naderi's web history, calling up each website that Nouri had visited and reviewing the content.

"Whoa . . .what's this?" Beth said.

Mark turned around and looked at Beth's large monitor. He thought to himself, "It's a cell phone—big deal."

"You gotta' see this. Naderi ordered three stun guns disguised as wireless phones. They're 700,000 volt stun guns."

Mark didn't even know such a thing existed. He bet that Homeland Security screeners at the airport didn't know it either.

Beth said, "Let's go back a few months and see if there's anything else."

After about an hour, Mark said, "I've found a bunch of YouTube videos of rocket explosions."

Beth said, "Yeah, I've got Naderi looking at Fuel/Air Explosive weapons."

Another two hours passed. "No way . . ."

"What've you got?"

"Nouri downloaded a Flight Simulator Program." Beth said. "I think we better talk to Sheryl."

Mark agreed.

Beth called Sheryl, "Do you have a couple of minutes?"

Welcoming the interruption since she was bored, Sheryl said, "Sure, come on in."

Mark and Beth explained what they had found so far. Sheryl asked, "When did you start monitoring the subject's Internet activity?"

"Back in September," Beth answered.

"So we have history starting at that point? How long will it take to go back and look at it all?"

"What do you think, Mark?" Beth asked, figuring about two weeks at least.

Mark answered, "I'd say about two, three weeks"

Sheryl said, "Too long."

Before Beth could protest, Sheryl added, "I'm putting two more teams on this. Beth, my wish is that you coordinate and get the information by Friday."

Beth said, as she stood to go, "That's doable."

By the next afternoon Beth had briefed the other special agents. They were eager to help. This was the first real threat many of them had seen since they began work in the unit. Beth had them start at the beginning, going over what she and Mark had found. After confirming what Beth had told them, the agents began finding other curious items. Nouri Naderi appeared to be interested in the Daytona Speedway and adjacent international airport. He had accessed satellite images, maps and other directional information from the Internet.

"Beth, I've got something here," said Mark.

Beth slid her chair over, looked and said, "Up to now I didn't think this was a serious threat, but this changes everything."

"Yeah, I agree. Nouri Naderi buys three one-way airline tickets out of the Daytona International Airport to Buffalo N.Y.," Mark said, thinking out load. "Wasn't Buffalo where that sleeper cell was located a few years ago?"

"They made several arrests as I remember"

Beth called the other agents over and showed them. "I need to know if there's anything significant about the departure date. Is it an anniversary of some terrorist attack or a special day in the Arab world or whatever?"

"What are you thinking?" one of the other agents asked.

"The date seems arbitrary. It's just a Sunday afternoon in February."

"We'll get right on it."

"See if there's anything on these other two names on Naderi's airline reservation," Beth told Mark.

A few minutes later Mark turned to Beth, "That was easy. Remember what started all this back a few months ago? There was a list of names from a radical mosque in Toronto and Naderi was on it?"

"Yeah."

"These other two guys, Farid and Reza Danesh belong to the same mosque. They're being monitored by a couple of Detroit special agents."

Beth thought for a few seconds. "You know, Mark, at this point I'd have a real concern if we were talking about these three subjects flying from New York, D.C. or some other large city. But what the heck is in Daytona Beach in February? Even the spring breakers aren't there until March. And, forget about Buffalo."

She got her answer almost immediately. Beth heard her named called and walked over to another cubicle. "It was right in front of us," said one of the other agents.

"What was?" She was looking at the Daytona International Speedway website.

"Look at the date of this year's Daytona 500."

"Oh, my God."

20

FTER WHAT BETH, Mark and the other agents
found, Sheryl thought it best to discuss the
situation with her boss, the special agent in charge.
They decided together that it was time to gather all the
agents involved for a meeting to assess the risk. It being
winter, Sheryl hadn't minded doing the extra work that
hosting the meeting would entail since it would be far
better than going up north. Jacksonville wasn't exactly
warm in January, but she thought it sure beat the
Detroit office where the other agents who were involved were located. She sloughed the work off on Beth
anyway.

When all the members arrived, they seated themselves around the long conference table. James Jetty,
PhD, a professor at NYU, also attended the meeting. He
was on retainer as an anti-terrorism consultant to the
Bureau. He was also a golfer, so he rarely turned down
an expenses paid invitation to Florida. Sheryl had

everyone introduce themselves and begin by asking Professor Jetty to give an overview of the current terrorist climate. Sheryl had heard his speech several times before, so she started drifting off. She looked around the room and it seemed strange that Beth's ex-partner wasn't there. Sheryl remembered another winter meeting like this one — almost four years ago now that she and Rob Jamison, Beth's ex-partner, had attended in Los Angeles. She also remembered vividly what happened. She thought of that time on many occasions.

After adjourning, Rob and Sheryl left for the airport together to catch a flight back to Florida. They were to connect in St. Louis and fly the remainder of the way back to Jacksonville. Because of a mechanical problem on the airliner, they were two hours late leaving. In the meantime, bad weather had moved into the St. Louis area, where a full-blown ice storm was in progress. The airplane sat on the icy tarmac for two hours; over the PA the captain told them several times that they were waiting for a gate and would only be a few more minutes.

When they finally got off the airliner Sheryl, like many other women on the plane, had an urgent need to use the restroom, and of course, there was a line-up. Rob said he would go find out if he could get them on another flight to Jacksonville that evening. However, there were no flights until noon the next day.

After the delay at the women's rest room, she found Rob, who told her that since all their troubles started with a mechanical problem, the airlines had arranged hotel accommodations for the night along with a meal voucher for him and would do the same for her. So Sheryl found herself in a huge line in front of the Passenger Service agent's counter. After another forty-five minutes, when it was finally her turn, they told her that they could arrange another flight for the next day, but all the hotel rooms were taken. The airline would of course reimburse her up to a certain dollar amount if she could find accommodations. Rob already had his hotel room, so he was all set, and she knew he wouldn't give his room to her. She figured that if she rented a car and drove a ways out of the area, she could probably find a room somewhere. Her flight wasn't scheduled to leave until the afternoon the next day, so she could drive a good distance if she needed. She remembered how mad she had been when she reached the rental car counter and was informed that because of the ice storm, all rental car companies would be suspending their operations. In other words, she couldn't get a car, and she didn't have a room. She looked around and by now there were individuals and families lying on the floor and many others trying to find any half-way comfortable spot to spend the night in the terminal.

Rob had a room, so she suggested that if he were a gentleman, he would give it to her, knowing the chances of that happening were slim to none. She was right again. However, Rob did suggest that she get on the hotel shuttle with him and try to intimidate the clerk into giving her a room by showing him her FBI identification. This sounded reasonable to her, and she thought it might work. However, the front desk clerk that night was a retired twenty-five year veteran of the St. Louis police force who had no love for the FBI. He even gave Rob the worst room in the hotel—and the place wasn't exactly the Four Seasons anyway.

She thought if she was a guy or with another female agent, it would be simple—just share the room. So figuring they were both professionals and this was an emergency she asked the question. Would Rob share the room with her? She remembered the smile on his face. Right then she knew it was a mistake, but she was screwed one way or another. If he tried anything, she was sure she would shoot him. There probably were two beds or at least a couch, although the thought of sharing a bathroom with him was alarming. When they got to the room, it was next to the elevator—tiny with one double bed, no couch and not even room for a roll-a-way. There wasn't even enough space to pull the mattress onto the dirty carpet. She remembered thinking to herself, "Could this get any worse?" And then Rob smiled again.

They dropped their bags and headed for the restaurant and lounge that was serving cold sandwiches until midnight, according to the clerk. The bar would be open until two A.M. They were both hungry so that's the direction they headed.

They had ended up closing the place. Sheryl didn't remember how many glasses of wine she had consumed, but it was a lot.

The next morning, it wasn't like the movies where the person wakes up to find they don't remember what they did and were surprised at whom they were with.

As soon as she opened her eyes, she knew exactly where she was, and she was pissed. Rob put his hand on her butt just then, and she shoved it away hard. She remembered the exact conversation.

"What's the matter with you?"

"You took advantage of me . . . you son of a bitch"

All she wanted to do now was to get as far away from him as possible. She looked around for her clothes and although the room was small, they were still out of reach. She didn't want him to see her naked. If she grabbed the sheet from the bed, then she would see him naked. She definitely wasn't about to wrap that skuzzy blanket around her either, so she just laid there angry and embarrassed. To make matters worse, she wasn't using any birth control, and he sure as hell hadn't used any protection. As she lay there, she said more to herself than as a question to him, "What if I get pregnant?"

"Then my kid will have a smart, beautiful mom," he said smiling.

She wasn't expecting an answer and certainly not that answer. Well, Rob got lucky that morning and many times thereafter.

21

SHERYL TUNED BACK into the meeting just as one of the Detroit agents asked Professor Jetty why only Muslims became suicide bombers. The professor said, "It's because those with other religions haven't been given permission yet."

The answer puzzled Beth so she and asked, "What do you mean, permission?"

"Let me offer this proposition to you. Do you remember the attack on the late Pope John Paul II, where he was shot by a Muslin man?"

Most everyone in the room nodded yes. "Well, suppose there was an attempt on the life of the current Pope, which was successful. Follow this act by savage attacks on Catholics and their churches. Given this situation, if the new Pope calls for 10,000 volunteers to be martyred to protect the faith, do you think he'd get them?"

"I think he'd probably get a 100,000 and half of them wouldn't even be Catholic," Mark said, getting a chuckled out of the group after the dry overlong lecture by the professor.

The professor said, "I know Special Agent Siene here is trying to add some levity to our serious conversation, but he isn't wrong. Under, the right conditions, things could get out of hand and we could have a Holy War."

"Like something out of the middle ages?" one of the agents asked.

"That's right. To many, dying for your country is a noble thing to do. People who do this are held up as heroes for their sacrifice. They may have volunteered for a mission knowing it was suicidal, and instead of being stopped, they end up being honored for their deeds."

"And rightly so," said Beth, thinking about her late husband.

The professor went on, "Now, isn't dying for your God, just as powerful for some people as dying for your country? It has its allure for many young men and women, but it's doubtful whether this notion of dying for your God is strong enough alone to have someone take their own life. There must be something else going on," Professor Jetty continued. "Let me use an analogy. How many of you are ex-military, or at least familiar with explosives?" Most of the hands in the room went up. "How many of you noticed that when handling these explosives, people aren't being all that careful, like loading a truck or a military cargo plane? How is this possible, without them blowing up themselves and their comrades?" asked the professor, pointing to one of the special agents.

"Well, the explosives we use today are stable without their detonators. Once a detonator is attached, they're handled a lot more gingerly."

"Exactly, dynamite without a blasting cap or another explosive without a detonator doesn't pose that much of a threat. Think of religion as that blasting cap. The detonator alone doesn't cause that much concern. It's only when you put it together with explosives that the danger increases dramatically."

"Well, what's the explosive part here?" asked the agent sitting next to Sheryl."

"Anyone here wish to take a stab at that question?" the professor looked around and saw that Beth had raised her hand. "Special Agent Cuddy. . ."

"Politics."

"Very good, Special Agent. Many Muslim countries in the Middle East have intertwined their religion with their government or political system. So an attack on their country is also an attack on their religion. Say an Israeli raid killed a young Palestinian man's brother when Israel was trying to stop mortar attacks on its citizens. The young man wants revenge and some deceitful cleric takes advantage of the situation. He tells the young man that not only is it proper to take revenge with his own life in a suicide attack against women and children, but he's protecting his faith. He will become a martyr for his efforts. There are countless examples through history. For example, the Kamikazes in World War II, where young Japanese men flew their planes loaded with explosives into our ships. Kamikaze means Divine Wind in English, and the emperor at that time was also Japan's spiritual leader. Religion mixed with politics can be a powerful motivator. Any questions?" asked the professor. "Good, let's say we take a ten minute break, and then I'm sure ASAC Niblock wants to get to the specifics of this meeting." It was close to tee time and the professor was anxious to be off to his golf game with the special agent in charge.

22

DURING THE BREAK MARK ASKED BETH, "Do you buy any of that?"

"It would explain some of the suicide bombings."

"No, I mean the stuff about the Pope."

"Who knows? I guess under the right conditions, it's possible. Even in the United States we've had bombings of abortion clinics for apparent religious reasons. True, they weren't suicide bombings, but that would be the next step." Beth said, sitting down. She could see that Sheryl wanted to get started.

It took about another hour for the special agents to present all the evidence. Sheryl said, "Alright, I'll brief the SAC this afternoon, so let me try to sum up what I've heard so far. We have three individuals who belong to a radical mosque in Toronto who bought one-way tickets to Buffalo from Daytona International Airport, which is adjacent to the Daytona International Speed-way. Their departure date and time coincides with the running of the Daytona 500 NASCAR race, which will have approximately 200,000 people in bleachers sitting out in the open. Correct so far?"

The group nodded, so Sheryl went on. "We have evidence that the subjects have shown an interest in aircraft explosions. They have purchased three stun guns, which appear to look like ordinary cell phones. By the way, have we ordered one of these ourselves?"

Beth said, "We're hoping it arrives today to see how realistic these things look."

"Good. Beth, it would be my wish that you contact Homeland Security to see if they can get the stun gun by the airport screeners, as a test."

Beth thought that was a good idea.

"So it's our view that these stun guns will be used to hijack an airliner and crash it into the Speedway spectators. Is that our conclusion?"

Most of the people in the conference room nodded except Beth and Mark. "You're not convinced," said Sheryl, looking at Beth.

"A few things don't fit. By the way, let me correct your summary in one area. The videos the subjects were watching were of rockets blowing up, not aircraft."

"Okay, what else?"

Beth said, "I've got some questions on timing. It doesn't seem to me plausible that there's enough time to hijack the plane while they're still in the Daytona Beach area. If the one-way trip was Buffalo to Daytona Beach, instead of vice-versa, it would make more sense. Also, we haven't found any reservations for hotels or car rentals, and we haven't determined how the subjects will get to Daytona Beach. Some things just don't fit."

"Well, things don't always fit exactly in any investigation," said Sheryl.

Beth thought that remark was somewhat condescending and continued with some irritation in her voice. "Also, we have no evidence that Nouri Naderi or either of the Danesh brothers have any real flight training other than the Flight Simulator software. It's inconceivable to me that any pilot would crash his plane into the crowd, no matter what the threat or coercion."

Sheryl didn't care for Beth's tone. "How many others share Special Agent Cuddy's concerns?"

Only Mark's hand went up and Sheryl said, "I think we want to characterize this as a hijacking attempt with the target being the Daytona Speedway. Here's our next step. I'll inform the SAC and Homeland Security. If the SAC agrees, I'll personally brief the locals." Sheryl was thinking that meant meeting with Milton Fryer, which she didn't relish.

"Beth, I want you to coordinate with our Ottawa office to see if we can get the subjects under surveillance. As I think about it, my wish would be that you go to Canada and supervise that effort personally," said Sheryl thinking that would cool Special Agent Cuddy off a bit. She smiled thinking about Toronto in February.

"I think we're done here for now."

Beth thought no matter what Sheryl was planning, she would continue to investigate. Something wasn't right. She could feel it. She smiled, thinking about

Sheryl sending her to Toronto. Beth knew why she did it, but she had actually done her a favor. Now she could personally watch Nouri Naderi and not have to count on coordination to get it done. As far as the cold, Beth grew up in Maine.

Beth went back into her cubicle ready to make travel arrangements to Toronto when her cell phone rang. The caller ID said it was her sister, Jeanne. Beth thought she never calls me at work. She answered, "Hi Sis, what's up?"

"Dad's in the hospital . . ."

At first Beth was confused. It was winter and her father lived with her in Florida.

"Dad collapsed on your lawn and your neighbor called the paramedics. My name was in his wallet as an emergency contact so that's why they called me."

"Is he alright?"

"No, he had an MI"

"What's an MI?"

"It's a heart attack."

"No! Where's Dad now?"

"He's at Memorial Hospital. I've talked to the doctors and told them I was a nurse. They told me that they think they have him stabilized. But they're checking for heart damage now. They promised to call me when they know more."

"I'm heading over there right now. Are you coming to Florida?"

"There's nothing I can do right now, but later on, he'll need care. I'll be down either Saturday or Sunday.

Mike's out of town til' Friday night, so someone has to care for the kids."

"I understand. I'll call you from the hospital and we can talk more."

Mark had heard most of the conversation and asked, "Is everything alright?"

"No, my father was taken to the hospital with a heart attack. Is Sheryl still here?"

"Yeah, I saw her on the phone."

"Listen, you'll have to take my place in Canada."

"I understand, I understand. Go see about your father. I'll tell Sheryl what happened."

23

MILTON FRYER, the mayor of Daytona Beach for the last six years, checked his voice mail. He had a message from Agent Sheryl Niblock. He found it strange that she wanted to set-up a meeting with him. It wasn't time for their twice yearly visits. He knew Agent Niblock didn't like him and he didn't care for her, either. Milton thought himself a good judge of bad character, and Agent Niblock seemed to fit that description.

Milton was anything, if not disarming. He knew when someone looked down upon him or judged him for his religious beliefs, and he was not above using that to his best advantage. He was not a good looking man. Milton had *Peter Rabbit* teeth and was slightly balding. He chose not to do anything about his teeth and actually smiled quite a lot. He figured this would take away from the one part of his appearance that those who spent a lot of time in his company frequently noticed— Milton Fryer had Charles Manson eyes. But in spite of his physical attributes, he was extremely popular with his flock. Mayor Fryer had perfect delivery. If he was more attractive, he might have chosen to be a television newsperson or an actor. He went into the ministry instead, and later politics—in his mind, two professions that were not so different.

He made it a point to annoy anyone who didn't care for him or his religious beliefs. He knew it was a character flaw on his part, but he couldn't help himself. Since Agent Sheryl Niblock certainly fell into this category, he would always have a little fun at her expense. Every time they were together, he would intentionally invade her space. He also did something that was the opposite of his normal behavior—quote Bible verses away from the pulpit. When he got carried away, Milton would actually make up a verse for the situation, attributing it to some non-existing apostle. Sheryl never ever noticed.

Milton called the number Sheryl had left and she answered on the first ring. After some pleasantries, she got right to the point. "Mr. Mayor, we may have a possible situation."

Milton thought this didn't sound good. He was busy with the biggest event in his city—the Daytona 500 and all that it entailed was coming up on Sunday, and he didn't have a lot of time for some bureaucratic nonsense. "What kind of situation?"

"There's a very slight chance of a terrorist attack," said Sheryl in her best monotone voice, trying not to illicit a fusillade of rapid fire questions that she couldn't answer.

"What in the hell did that mean", he thought. "Agent Niblock, are you trying to say that somebody is planning an attack on my city?"

Sheryl spent the next twenty minutes telling him everything her office knew so far—of course, leaving out how they obtained the information.

Milton would have a quarter of a million people visiting his city by Sunday afternoon and if word got out, it would be a disaster. Tens of millions of dollars in commerce would be lost—this on a *slight chance*?

"What are you doing about it, Agent?" asked Milton.

"We're watching the subjects closely, and we've asked the FAA to put more sky marshals on the aircraft entering and leaving Daytona Beach. We may ask them to halt air traffic to that airport during the race, but it's doubtful that they would comply without more concrete information."

"What can I do," asked Mayor Fryer.

"At this point, other than postpone the race . . ."

"Are you crazy?" he interrupted.

Milton figured this was nothing more than an attempt by Sheryl Niblock and the whole FBI, for that matter, to cover their respective asses if something did happen. They would say he was warned and didn't do anything about the threat. This would not stand. He said, "Let me get back to you, Agent," and hung up.

He wasn't going to start a panic. If he brought the city commissioners in on this, surely word would leak out. He might discuss it with the City Manager who he knew could keep a confidence. Besides, Sheryl Niblock assured him, the FBI had everything under control.

24

WHEN MARK ARRIVED midmorning at the Toronto airport, he was met by a special agent from the Ottawa Legat. The Legats were international legal attaché offices that the FBI maintained in about seventy cities around the world. These small offices made setting up operations like this much easier. Mark followed the special agent out to the curb where a van with electric company markings was waiting. He got in, looked around and said to the Canadian driver, "This is a lot nicer than what we have in the States."

The three men drove for a while until they came to a part of Toronto that was in transition—one of those areas that seemed to struggle between commercial and industrial. The driver, who hadn't spoken much since Mark entered the van, said in a Scottish accent, "I'll show you the layout before we park."

Mark could see what looked like an old gas station, but without pumps, facing a main street lined with small businesses. The Canadian driver, who by now Mark knew as Richard, said, "The Naderi son uses this old building for his motorcycle club. We see his friends come and go all the time. Last night we looked in the windows. The garage has an old SUV and is full of motorcycles. The office area looks like some kind of clubhouse. From what we could see, there's a big screen TV, leather couches and at least one computer in there."

To Mark, the building itself resembled an oversized service station similar to the ubiquitous quick-change lube businesses found on many commercial by-ways. It had large glass panel garage doors and probably a pit so workers could service the underside of the vehicles. He thought it looked big enough to fit three trucks.

"Is it a going business?" asked Mark.

"Not from what we can tell. The records show that at one time it was the main office of one of our big fuel companies based here in Toronto, which the Naderi family owns."

"So there's some money in the family, then?"

"It doesn't look like the family is strapped for cash," said the Canadian, driving off.

Anticipating his next question, Richard said, "We'll be relieving them. We've had people out here since yesterday.

The Canadian agent pulled over, and for the next two hours the three men took turns watching through the small window in back. A second surveillance van had moved into position about an hour after they arrived, and both were now watching the garage area. The Canadian's cell phone rang, "Yeah we saw them, two young men entering the garage. They didn't use a key, so we're assuming that someone else was already in there. They took a number of bags from their trunk before they headed in."

A few minutes later a late model luxury car pulled into the parking area on the far side of the building out of view from the office window. "That's Ali Naderi's car. He's the father."

A short time later another car, this one much older, pulled into the lot and parked next to the Naderi car. Mark watched as two men got out. The driver was a large man with a full beard. The passenger was a much smaller man, also with a full beard, but better kept. Ali Naderi got out of his car and greeted them. Then they walked behind the building.

About a half hour later, the other surveillance van reported that a garage window broke for no apparent reason. Richard asked, pushing the button to enable the speakerphone, "So it just shattered? We didn't see it."

"One pane of glass, near the top of the garage door."

"Did you hear anything?"

"No, but you know we can't hear much through these insulated vans. You think we should take a look?"

"Give it awhile. Let's see if anything happens on this side."

About fifteen minutes later, the man Mark saw earlier as the passenger, walked out from behind the building and then got into the driver's side of the car. "That's strange. He wasn't driving before."

The other two men in the van agreed. Mark said to Richard, "See if you can have one of your people take a quick look in the garage. If he gets caught, he can say he's looking for the electric meter."

Richard phoned over as the man they were watching seemed to be fiddling with the seat and mirrors. As he was driving away, Mark said, "Let's follow this guy."

A minute later the cell phone rang. "We have five men down!"

25

WHILE NOURI WAS IN THE CLUBHOUSE waiting for Farid and Reza, he had no idea the FBI and the Canadian authorities were outside watching. He also had no idea this was the last thirty minutes of his young life. Getting impatient waiting for his two friends, he thought he probably should've picked them up instead of having them meet at the building before leaving for Florida in the family's old SUV. While he was waiting there, Nouri was wondering why his father hadn't protested when he told him the Danesh brothers and he would be going to Florida to visit his brother Sami. His father had just nodded his okay.

While he was waiting, he phoned his brother who was in Tampa. When Sami answered Nouri said, "Listen, I was thinking it's probably not a good idea to call you on my cell phone once we leave Canada."

Sami said, "I agree. What are you going to do, pick up a throw-away when you cross over to the States?"

"I don't know yet, but don't plan on hearing from me for the next three days. I'll find a way to contact you, when we get there. Do you have all the stuff?"

"Yeah, I got everything except the liquid oxygen. I tested our little toy and it works fine."

"That's my brother, the electrical engineer." Nouri then heard his friends pull up, so he signed off.

Farid and Reza came into the clubhouse area with their bags. Nouri said, "Throw that stuff in the back of the SUV. I'll be right there. Let me shut down my computer and . . ."

The back door opened and his father along with Aram Danesh and Kasra Khatani walked in. The young men looked up in surprise and Nouri's father said, "You boys aren't going anywhere."

Ali Naderi picked up his son's notebook computer and walked into the garage area. The young men, still surprised, followed. Nouri's father seemed to be looking for something; he apparently found it. From the corner, Ali picked up an old sledgehammer and smashed Nouri's notebook into a million pieces. That's when Nouri heard the first loud bang, followed by many more. Nouri turned and couldn't believe it. He watched his friends fall to the floor just as Kasra Khatani was turning the gun on him. Nouri never felt it.

Kasra had shot everyone in the room at least once. But to his surprise, Farid wasn't badly hurt and jumped him. They grappled for the gun for at least a minute. Kasra was smaller and out of condition. Farid was a lot stronger than he looked. Kasra hadn't done anything like this for at least twenty years. His time in Canada had made him soft. He didn't have that revolutionary fervor that he could call on to give him that extra shot of adrenalin, that he needed in this situation. As they were wrestling for the gun, it went off, shattering one of the windows in the garage. Had the Canadian authorities investigated then, they may have saved Farid's life.

Just when he thought that Farid would get the gun away from him, the young man tripped over the sledgehammer, unbalancing himself enough for Kasra to pull away as Farid fell into the pit. Kasra wasted no time in shooting him.

Kasra Khatani walked around to make sure everyone was dead. It took another bullet to finish both Reza and Ali Naderi, who were unconscious, making that task somewhat easier. After the killings, Kasra took a minute to collect himself and think. He was to call his cohorts in Florida to let them know everything was all set on his end. He reached for his phone and remembered he left it in Aram Danesh's car. Aram lay dead on the floor. He liked Aram and the young men, but what had to be done, had to be done. He went back to the office area and saw a cell phone sitting on the table. Kasra figured, what's the difference. It was Nouri Naderi's cell phone. He looked through the address book for Sami's phone number. They forgot about that detail. The terrorists would need that information to contact Sami Naderi in order to get the supplies they needed. He called his co-conspirators and gave them the information.

Kasra then walked over to Aram Danesh and fished around in his pockets for the car keys. He would wipe everything down before he ditched the car. He went outside to the old auto and got in. It took him a minute to fix the seat. Aram Danesh was a much larger man, so he also had to adjust the mirrors before he left. As he drove off, he didn't see the electric company van pull out of its parking space a few blocks down the road.

Aram Danesh had picked Kasra Khatani up at his home that morning, but that's not where Kasra was headed now. His plan was to leave Aram's car in the long-term parking lot at the airport after wiping it down to remove any finger prints. Kasra would then take a shuttle to the terminal and a flight to Lebanon.

Mark Siene and the others followed Kasra Khatani to the airport parking lot. By now three other cars had joined them for backup. As soon as Kasra got out of the car, they jumped him, handcuffed him and brought him back to the police station for interrogation. Even without all the intrigue, the homicide of five people was enough to garner the attention of most of the Toronto police leadership.

26

SHERYL WAS BACK IN HER OFFICE. Mark had
left a few days before, after telling her about Beth's
father. Sheryl agreed that Mark should go to Canada in
his partner's place. She figured that Beth would be
taking some personal time to take care of her father.
Sheryl envied people with such close family connec-
tions. She was estranged from her own family.

Shutting down her computer, Sheryl was getting
ready to leave for the day when she realized that with
Beth gone and Mark already in Canada, she would have
to monitor TICS in their place. For some silly reason, the
FBI didn't allow special agents to access the system
outside the United States. Sheryl knew The Threat
Identification and Classification System had allowed
them to identify Nouri Naderi and the others and
determine what they were doing. But that didn't stop
her from hating the system, anyway. She would've been
aghast to know that her ex-husband had help design it.

Sheryl found it to be so boring, going through all those entries. Nonetheless, it was part of the job. She knew she had better at least glance at it to see if there were any new entries, but would get a cup of coffee first. Before she could leave her office, her phone rang. The caller ID told her it was her worthless real estate agent. "This is Sheryl."

"Sheryl, this is Sandi. I've got great news. We've got an offer on the condo."

Sheryl knew better than to get excited. The last time it was a low ball offer $40,000 less than her asking price.

"It's only $500 less than our listing price"

"Really?" Sheryl was completely surprised. The real estate market in the Jacksonville area, especially for condos, was still soft.

"There's a big contingency, though," her agent said.

Sheryl knew she shouldn't have let herself get too excited. "What is it?"

"They want a quick closing. It's a cash deal. You have to have your stuff out by Monday or they'll make an offer on one of the other Condos that's for sale in your complex. The guy's a Navy Captain who has to deploy and wants his family settled before his ship leaves. Apparently another deal fell through after a problem with a home inspection."

Sheryl didn't need the details. "Can we actually close that fast?"

"Yeah, we've done it before. It's not uncommon here in Jacksonville. Can you come on down to the office and okay the offer."

"I'm leaving now." Sheryl thought that was a surprise. That damn thing's been listed for months with only a few nibbles. Whatever she had to do to make this happen, she would do. So, she shut down the computer, knowing she could access TICS from home.

On her way to the real estate office, she started ticking off in her mind all the things she had to accomplish. If she was to close on Monday that meant she had to move all her stuff by Sunday. Since it was Thursday evening, and she hadn't done any pre-packing, it would be a busy weekend. She decided that she had to take Friday off. The mess with Nouri Naderi was contained. There was no way he or his friends would get aboard an airliner—never mind get into the country. That was for sure.

Sheryl Niblock spent all day Friday and Saturday packing. She managed to find a moving company that would move her belongings to a storage facility on Sunday. She was so busy that she hadn't realized she needed her computer to access TICS until she had already packed it. No matter, if she had time she would stop by the office on Sunday night after the movers left. What Sheryl didn't know was that a new entry for Nouri Naderi was flashing. It seems a call was made from Nouri's cell phone to an unidentified cell phone located in Daytona Beach. When Kasra Khatani called the two Hezbollah terrorists from Nouri's cell phone, they were scouting out the Speedway. That piece of information wouldn't be reviewed by anyone until early Monday morning.

27

A S SAMI FINISHED THE CALL with his brother, he realized they were really going through with this. Sami Naderi had started making preparations as soon as he returned to Tampa a few weeks ago. Since the spring semester didn't start for another week, it gave him a chance to do what he needed to do. He began work on the detonator first, which turned out to be much easier than he thought. A student on his campus had actually put plans on the Internet on how to use a children's remote control toy to set off a bomb. The authorities arrested the student for doing it, but once the information was out there, it was out there. He modified the basic design to use a cell phone instead of a controller because they needed more range.

Getting the parts also turned out to be easy. On the weekend he returned to Florida, there was a gun show in Tampa. He found a stun gun that he could use for $30, which he bought for cash. He then went to a local discount store and purchased a throwaway cell phone with the minimum number of minutes. That cost him another $75. The final stop was a hobby shop at the local mall where he bought a small electronics kit billed as *An educational experience for the young engineer.*

Since he didn't have any roommates, he built the detonator at his kitchen table. It was a simple device. All one of the young men would have to do was connect two leads and then turn the phone on. He glued the components to a cake pan and sealed everything except the electrodes to make the device watertight. He found some industrial strength double-face tape, which would hold the detonator to the bottom of the manhole lid. Sami was sure it would work. He tested it at least twelve times. Each time the phone rang, a 700,000 volt spark would jump between the two electrodes.

What turned out to be hard was the hydrogen peroxide in the strength that Nouri wanted. He almost gave up until he found a boat manufacturer that was going out of business and selling their equipment. They had gallons of the stuff, so he was able to buy what he needed.

The oxygen he knew he could pick up at a medical or welding supply house. So he would wait until Nouri and the others got there with the SUV.

The next couple of days were uneventful. Then as he returned from Friday afternoon prayers at a small local mosque in Tampa, he received a call on his cell phone. He wasn't expecting Nouri until the next day, and he didn't recognize the number that was on the display. When he answered, a man who spoke poor English, asked him if he spoke Arabic. Sami wasn't fluent, but he understood it much better than his brother. Speaking it was a different story. He expressed this to the caller, who said he understood better English than he spoke, so they decided Sami would speak English and the caller would speak Arabic. Sami asked what he could do for the caller.

"Can we meet somewhere?"

"Why?"

"I have a message from Kasra Khatani for you."

"Come by my apartment," Sami said giving the caller his address and directions. It turned out that the man was calling from a mall parking lot near campus.

About a half hour later he heard a knock and answered the door. Two men stood there, both unkempt and with some obvious personal hygiene problems. He invited them in anyway. Sami asked their names, and he thought they must have made them up by the way they answered.

"What can I do for you?" Sami asked, hoping they wouldn't stay long.

"Your brother and his friends won't be coming. Kasra Khatani discovered their plan and thinks it's far too dangerous. Khatani sent us instead. We will carry it out."

Sami reached for his cell phone but before he could use it . . .

"Do not call."

Sami thought about what he had just heard. It rather made sense. Despite their preparations, they had no idea what they were doing. Almost anything could go wrong and land them in jail, or worse. He was actually quite relieved. "Okay, I understand," he said.

"You will do for us what you planned to do for your brother. We will stay here for the night."

Sami thought these guys really need to take a shower, but he agreed anyway. Later, he asked them if they were hungry. They said yes, so he ordered some Chinese, which they said they liked. After about twenty minutes, he got in his car and went to get the food. On his way out of the parking lot, he noticed that they had driven to his place in a late model SUV with New York plates. When he returned home, something wasn't quite right. Many of his things were moved ever so slightly. Sami figured they must have searched the place. He checked. The money he kept in the ice cream container in the freezer was still there, and nothing else seemed to be missing.

Sami also noticed that the men had brought two bags not much larger than gym bags inside. After they ate the Chinese food, one of the two wanted to know if he had a washing machine in the apartment. Sami did, so he showed them how to use it. He also showed them where the towels where located if they wanted to take a shower. He was thankful they both took him up on his offer. His apartment reeked of Chinese food and sweat, so he opened the windows. He also used a half a can of room deodorizer, which helped a lot.

The next morning he took out the detonating device and instructed them on how to use it. They seemed to be impressed with his ingenuity and asked him if he'd done anything like this before. Sami knew better than to ask them the same question.

"We have to go and get the liquid oxygen this morning. These places are only open until noon on Saturdays."

"We go now," said one of the men in English.

They went out to the SUV and all three piled in the vehicle. Sami was expecting the car to smell, but surprisingly it didn't. He was happy about that. Buying the liquid oxygen didn't turn out to be as easy as he thought. The first place he tried was a medical supply house where he was told he needed a prescription for any type of medical gas. When he explained to the other men what happened, they weren't happy at all. The next place was a welding supply company, which did have what he was looking for. He paid and they drove around to the loading dock and put the containers in the back of the SUV.

The hydrogen peroxide was in the trunk of his car, so they didn't have to buy that. The men now wanted to see where Sami had planned to steal the truck. It was local, in the Port of Tampa area. They parked outside the chain link fence and watched for a good four hours. In the late afternoon they decided to head back. On the way, one of the men said, "Is there a place in the woods nearby where we can hide if something goes wrong?"

Sami thought about it. "There's a state park with a wilderness trail not too far from campus. It has a few cabins that people use when the weather's warmer."

"Show us this place."

It was almost dark when they got to where Sami had suggested. They pulled into the parking lot. There were no other cars.

"It's about a ten minute walk this way."

When they reached the cabin, they didn't go inside. The door was locked and they didn't have a flashlight. One of the men took out a 9MM pistol and shot Sami twice in the back of the head. The other felt around Sami's pockets, took his wallet and keys and left his body there.

28

AFTER THE TWO MEN killed Sami Naderi, they went back to his apartment for a good night's sleep. Early the next morning they awoke to a beautiful Sunday morning in Florida. It was unseasonably warm and not a cloud in the sky. After discussing the idea of setting Sami's apartment on fire to destroy any evidence that they had been there, both men decided it wasn't necessary. They didn't expect the authorities to apprehend them, let alone try them for murder. The men loaded the remainder of the supplies into the SUV they had stolen from a rental car company in New York.

On the way down to Florida, they laughed about how easy it was to get the car. The two men had bought green iridescent vests—the kind used by road workers or parking lot attendants—before going to the airport in Buffalo. They waited for a busy time, headed to the rental car return area, slipped on the vests and pretended to be lot workers. When they saw the vehicle they wanted, one of them directed the driver to a parking spot. The other asked whether he was returning. When the driver said yes, he helped him with his bags, wrote the mileage and fuel level on the paperwork then sent him on his way. The two men then got in the SUV and drove off—nobody the wiser.

They headed to the fuel distribution terminal—the one they had scoped out the day before. They reasoned that a full crew would not be working since it was Sunday. They were right. There was only one man in the yard, and he was busy filling a gasoline tanker. When he finished and moved the tanker truck to a parking spot, the two men pulled the same iridescent vest trick. They walked up to the worker, showed him the pistol then motioned him into the office area. During the week there would be ten or twelve administrative people working there, but today there were none. They ushered the yard worker into the women's restroom, figuring anybody who worked on Sunday would be male and nobody would find a body until the next day when the administrative staff returned. After they entered the restroom, they shot the yard worker in the back of the head then dragged his body into a stall.

When they went back outside, the men decided to prepare the truck before leaving. The larger of the two climbed to the top of the tanker while the other went to get the SUV holding the supplies. At first, the man on top couldn't figure out how to open the manhole cover. There were actually three. He tried them all and finally the middle one opened. The other man handed up the big brown bottles containing the hydrogen peroxide while the other poured them in. For some reason the yard attendant hadn't filled the tank all the way to the top, so there was about eighteen inches of room between the opening and the 14,000 gallons of fuel. The man climbed up the ladder with the detonator. He pulled the backing from the two strips of double-face tape and stuck the device to the bottom of the manhole lid. It fit perfectly. He attached the leads as Sami Naderi had showed him the day before and turned the phone on. All they needed to do now was open the valves and drop the two containers of liquid oxygen into the fuel. It was a good thing that the tank wasn't full to the top, because the two round containers didn't sink to the bottom as Nouri Naderi had predicted, but floated on top. The men were concerned that the two metal dewars would damage the detonator if they banged into it when they were driving. However when they were closing the lid, they noticed that the four inch rise where the lid attached would be just enough so the detonator wouldn't be damaged. Sami Naderi was smart to waterproof the device. The men were sure it would get wet. They closed the lid, climbed down and drove away, leaving the SUV in the yard.

The yard attendant had left the truck idling, so their departure wasn't delayed. The two men found their way to I-4 East and headed to Daytona Beach, making sure they didn't break any traffic laws. Two hours later, just before merging onto I-95, the driver noticed an official looking car behind them. It wasn't the black and yellow of a Florida State Patrol car, but it did have lights on the roof. They were wondering if it could be a local sheriff's car when the saw the lights begin to flash, apparently signaling them to pull over.

In the car was Officer Jim Bolton. He was driving one of the commercial vehicle enforcement units, patrolling for safety infractions. His job was to ensure commercial trucks and buses operating in Florida were mechanically safe, and the drivers had the proper license endorsements. In other words, ensure that the big trucks didn't create a safety hazard to the traveling public. He worked for the Florida Department of Transportation not the Florida Highway Patrol, but he had the authority to stop any commercial vehicle to perform safety inspections, enforce weight limits and make sure the drivers weren't under the influence of drugs or alcohol.

Office Bolton had just finished giving a citation to the driver of another big rig, and he was pulling back on the highway when he spotted a tanker truck with a damaged mud flap on the rear left set of tires. He wanted to make sure the remainder of the mud flap wouldn't end up being a projectile, possibly damaging another motorist's windshield or causing an accident with drivers trying to avoid debris in the road. So he turned his flashers on to signal the truck to pull over. When it didn't, he turned on his siren. When that didn't work, he pulled out from behind the truck came up to where the driver was located and used the PA to get the drivers attention. "Attention Driver. This is the Florida Department of Transportation. Pull your vehicle safely to the side of the road."

When the driver failed to comply, he tried his siren again, while blowing his horn. What came next he wasn't expecting. The driver swerved his truck into his lane. Officer Bolton avoided being hit, but nearly lost control of his cruiser. He pulled back behind the truck that had now picked up speed. He changed frequencies on his radio to FHP and called for backup.

The truck took the exit for I-95 North and almost didn't make it. The DOT officer estimated that the truck was going over eighty miles per hour. As soon as he entered I-95, two Florida Highway Patrol cruisers joined the chase and took the lead. When the truck exited at International Speedway Boulevard, it nearly tipped over as it merged onto the highway. The back of the tanker truck hit two cars, spinning both across the intersection. The first FHP patrol cruiser hit one of the spinning cars. The second continued to give chase.

After about a half mile, the trooper still following the truck noticed it was slowing down, thinking the driver was finally pulling over. Instead, the truck turned right into the Daytona Speedway parking lot, smashing cars as it tried to make the tight turn. The trooper followed the truck into the parking lot, watching the big rig hit at least twenty more cars as it made its way along the back of the grandstands. Finally, it stopped near the large tower area. The trooper got out of his cruiser, drew his weapon and . . .

29

BRANDON MCBRIDE JR., a young maintenance worker, was standing on the roof of the high-rise hotel that had a good view of the Daytona International Speedway. It was a slow day since most of the guests were at the track watching the race. He had a camcorder set-up on a tripod and was hoping to capture some exciting video that he could upload to the Internet. The camcorder was a Christmas gift from his parents and it could zoom to 35X with its telephoto lens. So far, he had not captured anything that wouldn't be shown on TV.

He was almost ready to pack it up and go back inside. The sun was setting and he figured the glare was affecting the quality of the video. As he was reaching for the camera he noticed activity in the Speedway parking lot. A big tanker truck seemed to be out of control and was smashing into the parked cars. He swung the camcorder around to capture the scene as the truck plowed into the chain link fence that kept spectators from going under the grandstands.

The blast knocked Brandon down. He lay there realizing that the windows had shattered below him. His ears were ringing. But incredibly, the camcorder was still on the tripod. After he picked himself up he had the presence of mind to continue filming. As he moved the camera around he started to narrate what he was seeing. He didn't realize it then, but over the next few years, hundreds of millions of people would download it from the Internet, see his video, and hear his voice.

The young man zoomed out and began his recitation, "There's a huge fire. I can't see the stands. The flames are blocking my view. I hear people screaming. This is terrible! The smoke is blocking out the sun. I'm not sure how much of this I'm getting. I'm going to keep talking. Let me zoom in here—holy shit, there are people on fire! The racecars are smashing into pit row. What was that? A piece of burning wreckage just fell ten feet from me."

Brandon picked up the tripod and pointed the camcorder to the material burning on the roof. He put the video camera back down, and he stomped out the flames. "There's burning stuff falling all over the place. Cars are exploding in the parking lot. The people can't get by. Ooh, that's bad! I don't know how much more of this I can watch. I see some people are making it out. They're running onto Speedway Boulevard. The flames don't seem to be letting up. Lots of people must be dead!"

He watched for another fifteen or twenty minutes, then took the stairs down to the first floor lobby. He went outside to get a closer look. Many people were moving in his direction; he had to look away.

The glass was still falling to the ground from many of the broken window frames, and it was dangerous to remain where he was standing. He went back into the lobby area and thought about somehow securing the first floor broken windows so thieves would not have easy access. Then Brandon had an idea. With all the activity, nobody would notice if someone did climb into the windows and rob the guest rooms. He looked around—he could see no other staff so he used his pass card to enter each guest room. Brandon methodically did a search of each guest room, knowing where someone might try to hide their valuables. He was major league successful and recovered quite a haul. Brandon collected his loot and thought about doing the same thing on some of the upper floors, but decided against it. Why be greedy he thought. He had principles.

30

AS MAYOR MILTON FRYER would say many years later, it was literally for the grace of God that he wasn't killed that day along with most of the other city leaders. Milton, as a former preacher, followed all the commandments religiously except for the last one, "Thou shall keep holy the Sabbath day." It was almost impossible to avoid doing the city's business on Sundays. If he left the house, he would invariably meet someone who wanted to discuss one civic matter or the other. He made a concession to this indiscretion during lent. For the five Sundays leading up to Easter, he wouldn't leave the house after he and his family returned from the church service. Because Easter came early this year, the Daytona 500 race was on one of those Sundays. He had attended many of the other Speed Week races and events, so most people probably wouldn't miss his absence.

After a nice Sunday dinner with the family, he relaxed with his son-in-law, watching the new high definition television set that his children had chipped in to buy him as a Christmas gift. As they watched the Daytona 500 race, the corner of the screen showed Lap 121 of 200 as the racecars moved around the track. Then the screen went blank. His first thought was "what happened?—this is a brand new TV." They didn't hear the noise of the explosion six miles away for almost half a minute. The house literally shook on its foundation when the sound, traveling at 1,100 feet per second, did reach them. Milton and his son-in-law ran out to see what was happening. They didn't have a clear view because of the surrounding homes—and at first didn't see anything. They walked quickly to the end of the street where the intra-coastal waterway separates their barrier island neighborhood from the mainland. Then they saw it! A huge black plume of smoke covered most of the southwestern sky, blotting out the setting sun. At first Milton thought it was a plane crash since it was near the airport, but it looked to large for that. He ran back to the house and grabbed his cell phone. He speed-dialed the emergency tactical telephone number, which was supposed to be monitored 24 hours a day. It took fourteen rings before someone answered.

"This is Mayor Fryer, who's this?" he asked since the person answering didn't give his name.

"Sergeant Robles, sir."

"What's going on?"

"There's been an explosion, sir."

"I know that, that's why I'm calling," the mayor said, starting to get impatient. "Where? What happened?"

"We're getting reports that there's been a huge explosion at the Speedway. Hold on a second . . ."

The mayor thought, "Oh God."

"Sir, we have a bird in the air and they're saying it's bad"

"Can you patch me through directly to the helicopter pilot?"

"Hold on, sir"

It took about 20 seconds before the pilot responded, "Mr. Mayor, are you there, over?"

"Officer, switch to cellular transmission." Many people monitored the police frequencies, mainly the media, and he didn't want to be overheard.

After a couple of minutes, listening to an insane description of what was happening, the picture on the TV returned, showing the scene. Apparently, an aircraft of some kind was shooting the video. The pictures were even worse than what the helicopter pilot was telling him.

He said to the pilot, "I've got to get over there."

"Do you want us to come get you?"

"No, I don't want you off station."

"Sir, I don't think you can get here by car. The blast knocked out most of the power in the area, and many accidents happened when the traffic lights went out. It's a mess," said the helicopter pilot.

"Thanks, officer. I'll get back to you," said the mayor.

Milton thought for a second, then decided what he would do. Daytona Beach was home to Bike Week and

Biketoberfest, two of the largest gatherings of motorcy-cles riders in the country. You didn't get to be mayor of the city if you couldn't ride a motorcycle. He had a Harley-Davidson Police Special in his garage that he rode up and down Main St. during these events. It was fitted with a siren, flashing lights and police communi-cations. He quickly changed his clothes, strapped on his helmet, plugged in the communications gear and then started the bike. He used the police radio to contact the helicopter pilot for guidance on the best route.

Everything was fine until he crossed the bridge. Then everything was completely blocked. The city had modified its curbs located at intersections for handicap access, so he was able to drive the motorcycle onto the sidewalk, up one ramp and down another. Milton did this for several miles. It was slow going with the big heavy motorcycle, but he was making progress until . . .

Heading for him, was a wave of humanity, a huge crowd. As he got closer, he was horrified. The head-lights from the stopped traffic reflected on people; some were bloody; all were filthy with soot. Many had streaks on their cheeks where the tears had washed the soot away. It was obvious most were hurt or in shock. He wondered where they were going. Thank God, there weren't many children in the crowd. This was bad enough. Milton called the helicopter again and asked about the people. The pilot told him it was the same in all directions leading away from the racetrack, and the throngs of people didn't seem to be heading for any particular place, just away from the tragedy.

Milton made his way along the next half mile the best he could. He finally abandoned the motorcycle and fought the zombie-like pack moving in the opposite direction. Milton saw an eerie orange glow in the western sky and thought to himself that it was like something you would see on the National Geographic Channel when they showed pictures of an active volcano at night. Milton came upon a police cruiser stuck in the traffic jam, surrounded by people crying out to the officer for help. The beleaguered sheriff's deputy looked scared, as if the crowd was trying to attack him. The mayor was now as far as the shopping mall parking lot that stood across the street from the Speedway. People were lying on the ground—some with terrible burns, waiting for medical assistance. Many were bleeding from the ears and some were wandering around blinded, calling for help. Although the lights were out and it was now after 8:00 P.M., he could see all this because of the hundreds and hundreds of cars that were burning in the Speedway parking lot and the main fire was still throwing flames 200 feet in the air. He wondered how these poor people could have made it even this far.

Milton found his way over to the motel next door to the mall, which had a decent size parking lot in the rear that, for some reason, was almost empty. He called the helicopter pilot for a pickup. In less than two minutes he was in the air. The horrors of what he had seen over the last two hours were nothing compared to what he was seeing now. "Oh, my God", he mouthed.

31

BETH WAS SITTING in her father's hospital room,
watching him eat his dinner. She thought he looked much better and his appetite seemed to be good. The
little TV attached high up on the wall opposite the bed
was on, but she wasn't paying much attention. It was
some kind of car race. She saw her father look up in
surprise. The TV was showing a huge fire. "Dad, where
is that happening?"

"Daytona, the Speedway's on fire."

"What?" Beth listened to the newsperson describing
the events. She heard the words *possible terrorist attack*.
She knew right away that this had something to do with
Nouri Naderi and his gang. She continued listening and
didn't hear anything about a plane crash. Beth grabbed
her cell phone and called the duty officer at the FBI
office. It was standard procedure, in case of emergency,
for the duty officer to have instructions for the special
agents. However, in this case she told Beth she would

get back to her. While Beth's father continued to watch the horror that was unfolding, she went down to the nurse's station. An informal meeting was taking place. Beth heard bits and pieces of the conversation. They were discussing triage. Apparently, Homeland Security had informed the hospital to expect a multitude of casualties—the hospital had to make as many beds available as soon as possible. The doctors at the station were telling the nurses which patients to discharge early. Beth heard her father's name.

Beth thought it was a good thing her sister was on her way to Florida. She had already arranged for her children's care and would arrive later that evening. Beth was supposed to pick her up at the airport in Jacksonville. Beth knew it was going to be busy for her in the FBI office—and to add taking care of her father at home, also, would be impossible. In Beth's mind, family came first. With her sister coming it wouldn't be a problem, though.

About three hour later, while her father was getting his last good going over by his doctor before the hospital discharged him, Beth headed down to the lobby. The duty office still hadn't called back with instructions. When the elevator door opened on the ground level, it was bedlam. There were gurneys all over the place, holding intravenous bottles. People were crying out everywhere she looked. The hospital had run out of pain medication and new arrivals were suffering terribly. Many people had horrible burns and some were missing limbs. She hoped her father didn't have to witness this when they left. She heard one of the paramedics tell a doctor that it was like this in every hospital from Jacksonville to Orlando. He also said that they weren't answering any emergency calls from the local area. They were sending all equipment to Daytona Beach. "If the heart attack had happened today, my father would have died," Beth thought to herself. She found out later that was just what had happened to quite a few other people. For the next thirty hours, if you have a medical emergency, you're on your own, she heard the paramedic say.

Two hours later, Beth was back at her home. Her sister had called from the airport wondering why Beth hadn't picked her up. She explained the situation to her sister and suggested she take a taxi. In the meantime, the duty office had finally called her back. "All special agents should report to the office by 5:15 tomorrow morning."

Beth had the news on and they were reporting that the authorities still hadn't ruled out a nuclear attack. The networks had footage of panicked people on the West Coast of the United States, which was three hours behind them, mobbing grocery and other stores that were still open. People were emptying the shelves. Beth figured the same would go on tomorrow in her city, as well as every other city in the United States. She knew it wasn't a nuclear attack, so it was important to get the word out as soon as possible, and this would be part of her job. By now it was almost midnight and she knew she wouldn't get to sleep. "Sis, I'm going to the office."

"Now?"

"Will you be alright here with Dad?"

"I'll be okay. I can use Dad's car to get his prescriptions tomorrow."

The pharmacy at the hospital had been too busy to fill the prescriptions that night. Beth hoped that her sister wouldn't have any trouble the next day. She had already warned her sister about the lack of emergency help.

Beth got in her car and headed for the office. When she arrived most of the other special agents were already there. She knew Mark was still in Canada. Curiously, she thought, Sheryl wasn't there, but Sheryl's boss was in his office with some people she didn't recognize.

32

THE FAA HALTED all commercial flights going into the adjacent International Airport. The United States Government, having learned their lesson during Hurricane Katrina, was trying to respond as quickly as possible. The government was flying in medical, rescue and recovery personal from all parts of the country. This help started arriving within six hours following the blast, but because of darkness and damage, they had to wait for first light to begin their efforts. Luck had changed a bit at sunrise, when an east wind caused the thick black smoke that had been obstructing the sun to scatter, allowing a clear view of the racetrack area. However, many responders that day probably would have preferred that it wasn't so clear, since even hardened veterans of the Iraq and Afghanistan conflicts had not seen anything even remotely like this. There were thousands and thousands of charred body parts covering the area. Many of those still alive had suffered horrible burns and were crying out in pain. Hundreds of people were wandering around calling out for their relatives. The stench of burnt flesh and rubber, as well as bodily fluids and chemical odors, would cause anybody to gag. And, many of the rescue people did vomit at the sights and smells.

Milton and with what was left of the city's leadership setup a command post at the air terminal next to the Speedway. The governor, several members of FEMA, and Homeland Security had arrived, and they were all trying to organize the effort. The blast had killed the people who would normally be responsible for this task including the police and fire chiefs and many of their senior officers, so the group wasn't making much progress. There was a lot of bickering because each person had his or her own idea about what they should be doing. Finally, Milton Fryer had enough. He appointed himself police and fire chief. Although, it was a bureaucratic move, it did the trick. The police and fire department personnel started following his orders. The governor in time, relinquished control of the National Guardsmen to the mayor as well.

That morning the only way to get the injured out of the area was by helicopter. The streets around the Speedway were still impassable, but it didn't matter anyway. Every emergency room and urgent care facility within 50 miles was jammed with the walking wounded. Helicopters were flying the injured to Orlando, Jacksonville and as far away as West Palm Beach hospitals.

Tents erected for a triage area were already at capacity and they still had not removed a third of the injured. In the next few days the rescuers started converting many of the area hotels to makeshift hospitals. During the night, bulldozers and other heavy equipment working on the runway construction project, along with the airports firefighting foam trucks, had made their way over to the nearby Speedway and had extinguished many of the car fires. The main blaze had finally burned itself out, incinerating or melting everything in its wake.

Milton Fryer thought, thank God for the Red Cross and Salvation Army as well as the other volunteers. They set up their facilities at the mall whose stores were closed due to the power outage and early hour. They were feeding the people and offering comfort as well as collecting information.

In order to get a handle on things, Milton had instructed all the city's department heads who were still alive, to contact all local hotels within a 60-mile radius of the Speedway. Since it was now Monday morning, the hotels would be waiting for the race fans to checkout. Many would not be doing that since they had been killed or injured in the attack. The mayor figured it would be a good way of getting a rough count of the missing. By noon, that task was mostly completed.

The media had finally come to their senses. News directors were now exhibiting some restraint in the images they were broadcasting. However, this restraint didn't extend itself to reporting rumor, speculation and in some cases, downright falsehoods. It would be several days before the full facts were known and the recriminations began. Around the nation there was still a good deal of panic. The mushroom cloud of smoke caused some media to report erroneously that it had been a nuclear explosion, and many people were afraid that there was more to come. It took thirty-six hours for the authorities to confirm that there was no radiation and the weapon, whatever it had been, was conventional in nature. However, in those thirty-six hours panic shoppers mobbed every supermarket from Florida to California. People were behaving badly, and the police were reporting looting in some areas.

Wall Street suspended trading, fearing a huge sell-off like what happened during the 9/11 attack. Customers were overrunning bank lobbies wanting cash from their accounts. There were long lines at every ATM in the country, at least those that still were dispensing cash. Many gas stations had run out of fuel, and those that were still operating had cars lined up for blocks. The home improvement stores had a run on plastic sheeting and duct tape, which was puzzling, and portable generators. Long distance calls to the Florida area were almost impossible—people were hearing recorded messages to try their parties later. Many companies had to shut down for the day when workers did not show up because they were out buying supplies or watching the events unfold on television.

33

THE SEVEN MEMBERS of the new Iranian Ruling Council, formerly the senior commanders of the Revolutionary Guards, were meeting to consider whether Iran's former president should be included in their ruling body. Since the bloodless coup several months earlier, where they deposed the supreme leader, the Ayatollah Kasmani, along with the entire Council of Guardians, the commanders now met regularly. The chief commander said, "We have discussed this matter enough. The president was a loyal member of the guard before taking office and a friend to us afterward. I say we should let him join us."

The others in the room nodded their assent.

"Then it is done. He is waiting outside. Let us invite him in. There are other matters for us to discuss."

One of the less senior generals opened the large door and invited the former president into the room. They told him he would keep his title of president, but the chief commander who was now head of their council had the real political power.

After a number of government matters where discussed, they summoned an aide to bring in a television set so the council could see the latest developments on the Muslim streets regarding the Daytona Speedway attack. The Western media, not wanting to inflame the American people, showed little of the demonstrations. People in the United States had no idea of the effect that the events in Daytona Beach was having on a large part of the Muslim world. However, Arab television was showing it all. The aide found the correct channel and the council members began to watch the coverage. Between clips of damage and devastation, the pictures were showing celebrations in many Muslim countries. People were dancing in the streets, tossing homemade dummies into large piles, and setting them afire. The commentators were saying that there appeared to be a general sense of glee in many Muslim areas. The TV reporting also told of government leaders making statements, trying to lessen the enthusiasm in their countries. There was also some video showing the police breaking up the demonstrations with force. Some commentators speculated that this was no doubt an attempt to appease the government of the United States, rather than a real sense moral outrage.

The ruling council members knew there were crowds in their own streets chanting death to America and other insults. A huge protest was currently taking place in Hafte Tir Square where tens of thousands had gathered. The demonstrations had been going on for hours and the now the council was to decide what they should do.

"I say let them continue," said the Iranian president.

"I agree. Look at all these so-called leaders kowtowing to the Americans. Even Syria is chasing people off the streets.

"The Americans deserved everything they got. Why are not these words being uttered in their speeches? All we hear are condolences. It is sickening."

"What should be our position?" asked the chief commander to the group.

"Encourage our demonstrators. Prove to the world that Iran is not scared of the Americans and their saber rattling. I say we go out there and join them," said the former president, which was in character with his normal belligerency. "We can show them the real leaders in the Muslim world."

"What about the American response?"

"What will they do? There's no proof that we had anything to do with the attack. They'll eventually find out who the actual attackers were, but there is no tie to anyone in Iran."

The other men in the room all thought about the president's statement. He had not been party to the discussion they had month's earlier. He wasn't a member of the ruling council when they had decided to back Hezbollah.

"I agree the Americans won't attack us. They're still licking their wounds from there experience in Iraq and Afghanistan," said another council member.

"What about the reaction from the rest of the world? They're already mad at us over our nuclear program."

"They won't do anything. They need our oil."

"So we agree to let the protests go on the way they are?"

"No. I think we should organize them to get maximum coverage from the media."

"What do you want to do?"

"It has to be outrageous—something totally unexpected that hasn't been done before. Otherwise it is just more pictures of the same. The networks will get bored with it and move on to one of their scandals they like so much."

"I agree. We have to show the world that we are not afraid of the Americans. We want the rest of the Muslim countries to follow us. We must get them involved somehow or we will again be painted as pariahs and dismissed out of hand."

"What about bringing their people to our streets?"

"What do you mean?"

"Invite the most militant of them to rally in Iran. If enough of their citizens come to Tehran, their weakling governments will be too afraid not to follow us."

"You think they will fear their people returning and toppling them?"

"I believe so."

"That could work," said the chief commander. "Let us think about it. But first, we should go out and show our own people that we support them." He got up to join the protestors, and the other seven men followed him.

34

S HERYL SAT AT HER DESK with her head in her hands, wondering what had happened. They thought they had the situation contained. Earlier, her boss knowing most of what Sheryl knew, had related to the deputy director the facts as they knew them. The Deputy then relayed the information to the Director who would brief the president. The president of the United States was to address the American people that evening and wanted as many details as was known. Sheryl kept looking at the preliminary casualty figures FEMA was providing. It was almost unfathomable. The authorities on the scene estimated the initial blast had killed about 23,000 people, another 41,000 died within the next thirty minutes and according to the medical authorities, more than 14,000 would eventually succumb over the next several weeks. An additional 40,000 were hurt badly, some with serious, disfiguring injuries. Medical personnel were moving the injured to hospitals all over the country. The blast destroyed the entire VIP spectator section killing local dignitaries, 32 members of congress, a network anchorperson as well as other celebrity race fans. Most of this death toll was based on the number reported missing, since counting bodies was nearly impossible. FEMA hoped that maybe some of the missing would reappear, but nobody was very optimistic. Sheryl thought 118,000 people killed or injured. That was more casualties than the Hiroshima nuclear bomb blast.

Sheryl got up to see if Beth was making any progress. She'd returned to work after being reassured that her father would recover.

Mark Siene had already filed his report about the events that took place in Toronto. So they already knew that neither Nouri Naderi nor his friends were directly involved in the attack. Mark called earlier and said that the questioning of Kasra Khatani was still underway.

Sheryl walked to Beth's cubicle and apparently startled her when she called her name. Beth turned and gave Sheryl a look of disgust, which seemed to Sheryl as an overreaction and totally uncalled for. At first, she figured Beth was pissed because she had surprised her, but Beth continued to glare at her.

Sheryl said, "What . . .?"

Beth pointed to something on TICS. Sheryl, not wearing her contacts and forgetting her glasses in her office, had to get cheek to cheek with Beth to see the monitor. It was uncomfortable for Sheryl, and Beth wasn't giving away any space. Beth was pointing to a phone call icon on Nouri Naderi's corkboard, time-stamped four days earlier. Sheryl started to get a tightening feeling in her stomach.

Beth was so angry her hands were shaking, causing her to hit the wrong part of the icon, which in turn allowed the women to hear a short conversation in what Sheryl recognized as Arabic. From the previous briefings, she knew that Nouri Naderi was Canadian, so he spoke English and French, as well as Farsi, because of his family's connection to Iran. She wasn't told he also spoke Arabic. Beth hit the correct symbol and brought up the translation. It was obviously a coded message of some kind and digits of a phone number with a 386 area code. Beth then hit the symbol showing the GPS locator. The call originated from a cell tower close to Nouri Naderi's residence and was received in Daytona Beach. Sheryl gasped. She knew right away she had missed it and why. Beth knew it too.

35

BETH HAD FINALLY CALMED herself down. She
knew the significance of the call, but she was puzzled. Over the past few months she had listened to
many of Naderi's telephone conversations, all of which
were in English. However, even in Arabic, it didn't
sound like Nouri's brother, Sami. So Beth requested a
voice analysis through TICS. If anything was on record
to identify the speaker, it would come through in a few
days. A few minutes later, her cell phone rang. The
caller ID said it was Mark who was still in Canada. She
answered.

"I'm waiting here and I'll be watching the interrogation. Should I let Sheryl know what I'm doing? I called
her this morning."

"No Mark, I'll handle it"

Beth got up and walked to Sheryl's office, which was
two doors down from the special agent in charge. As
she walked by the SAC's office, the blinds were not

totally shut on the glass wall, so she could see Sheryl standing in front of his desk. She couldn't hear the conversation, but by the look on the SAC's face, he didn't seem to be treating her kindly. Beth figured that Sheryl had tried to mitigate the damage to her career by attempting to get in front of her apparent dereliction of duty before the SAC found out another way. Beth lingered long enough to see Sheryl place her sidearm on the SAC's desk. Sheryl then tossed the case containing her badge and ID next to the gun. Beth thought that although Sheryl was the first to go down, she wouldn't be the last. But the SAC would keep the wolves at bay for a few days with Sheryl's departure.

Beth waited until Sheryl left before knocking on the SAC's door. She didn't let on that she knew what had happened to Sheryl. She told him she couldn't find Sheryl, and there were some new developments. Would he like to hear them? After finishing the update, he asked her if she had heard from her ex-partner recently, and she said she had. The SAC wanted her confidential opinion on whether she thought Rob Jamison would come out of retirement and take Sheryl's position on a temporary basis. It was less than a year since he had left the Bureau after losing-out on a promotion to Sheryl. Beth ducked the question, but suggested that the SAC call Rob.

When Beth returned to her desk, she was surprised to find that her request for voice analysis was already completed. Mossad had a file for the person in Daytona Beach who had received the call from Nouri Naderi's phone. It turned out to be a former member of Hezbollah. The organization had kicked him out as being too fanatical for even that radical group. The Mossad's dossier said he had strong ties to Iran, and he was suspected of several bombings in Lebanon. Beth started thinking. She called Mark who was still working with the Canadian authorities. "Mark, do you know about what time, the Khatani left the Naderi property?"

Mark gave her the exact time, which was about three minutes after the call was placed on Nouri's phone. Beth told Mark what she knew and Mark would follow-up during the interrogation.

36

BETH'S EX-PARTNER and now her new boss, Rob Jamison, reflected on how much had changed for him personally and for the entire country in the last three weeks. His net worth had plunged about 30 per cent after the Speedway attack since his retirement account had consisted mostly of aggressive growth stocks, which took a beating. He depleted most of his liquid holdings, namely his money market account, during his extended vacation after leaving the FBI. He wasn't in deep financial trouble like many of his elderly retired neighbors who were suffering after the bottom fell out of financial markets, but he was hurt, nonetheless. So when the Jacksonville SAC called and offered him a temporary position as ASAC for Counterterrorism, he swallowed his pride and took the job. Actually, he thought, he didn't have to swallow too hard, as he grabbed a shirt from the bedroom closet he now shared with Sheryl.

Since Sheryl had sold her condo and then resigned from the FBI, she had no place to go. She was estranged from her family, so she asked if she could move in with him temporarily. Everyday he returned home, he found more and more of Sheryl's personal belongings replacing his. She boxed his things up neatly and placed them in his large garage.

Rob didn't live too far from the office and that was a good thing. Fuel was hard to come by since Homeland Security overreacted and required all fuel trucks to have a police escort for their deliveries. The scheduling nightmare could have been prevented had they anticipated it. Trucking companies had to coordinate their deliveries with the police agencies without any efficient method in place to do it. The result was massive fuel shortages in many parts of the country, and Florida was no exception. Drivers had to wait up to four hours for gas and there was a ten gallon maximum on fuel purchases. The country had not seen anything like this since the Carter Administration, when he was a teenager, and a third of the United State's population hadn't yet been born.

On Rob's first day back to work he saw many agents he hadn't seen in years. He wasn't the only one called back. Mosques all over the country were vandalized, shot at, and a few even bombed since the incident at the Speedway. The FBI was swamped helping the local authorities investigate these crimes. Deep down, although he would never admit it to anyone, he could see how these individuals could come to do this. Every night the cable news networks showed people dancing in the streets in the Middle East and Iran, celebrating the recent tragedy. News clips showing big crowds of demonstrators in Iran, people holding up their signs in English calling for death to America, had a different meaning to many people now.

Rob picked up the phone in his office and called Beth. He would protect her if he could when the axes started swinging. He needed and trusted her; they were friends. When she answered, "Yes, Boss," he heard her say the word boss with affection. Rob knew it wouldn't last once Beth found out whom he was living with. "Do you have a couple of minutes?"

"Sure, I'll be right over."

Beth entered the office that had recently belonged to Sheryl. She could still smell Sheryl's expensive perfume. "What do you need?"

"Let's talk for a second. I had a chat with the SAC today, and he told me that Sheryl never mentioned your concerns about the attack not coming from an airline hijacking. She told him that the group was all onboard with the theory."

"Did you set him straight?"

"Yeah, the SAC's known Sheryl for a long time, so he didn't doubt it for a minute. He knows about your father and how Mark was out of the country. I don't think there will be a problem, but there will be an investigation. Sheryl's the only one on the hook for this right now. But to be fair, even if we did know about the phone call, we still didn't know how they were going to do it."

"I guess that's true."

"As I see it, the real screw-up was not having the Naderi brother in Tampa under surveillance."

"We knew about him, right?"

"Yeah, we knew about him. He was on the same list of mosque members that the others were on"

"When Sheryl had the Detroit agents down here for that risk assessment meeting, were the Tampa agents invited?"

"Sheryl had me arrange the meeting. I invited them personally. They declined; said they already talked to Sami Naderi three times on campus."

"Were they briefed about what you guys decided?"

"I don't believe so."

"So they had no concept of the threat?"

"I guess not."

"So much for connecting the dots . . ."

"I see what you mean about where the real screw up was. If we were following Sami Naderi, we would've been on to those mutts, also."

"Maybe—at least we would've had a better chance."

"So Sheryl really isn't to blame, then?"

"Well, I won't exactly say that. She did less than a stellar job. Listen, tell me about Mark Siene."

"Mark's a good guy—very detail oriented. Sometimes he tries too hard with the 'people-person thing', but I like him. He's amiable . . ."

"Can I trust him?"

"Yeah"

"Good. I think its time for an update from the group. Can you put it together? How about you get everyone together in the conference room later?"

"OK, I can do that."

37

B ETH ASSEMBLED THE AGENTS investigating the attack in the conference room in less than an hour. Since this included most of the special agents in the Jacksonville office, there wasn't a seat left at the table. They brought in more chairs and lined them up against the walls. She watched as Rob walked in, looked around, and then walked out again. She followed him.

He said, "Are you kidding me?"

"Too many people?"

"I don't want to see more than eight people in that conference room. It's a circus the way it's set-up." Rob paused and smiled, "My wish is . . ."

Beth laughed. She hadn't been doing a lot of that lately. "I'll go in and organize this better. We can reconvene in about an hour?"

"Good, go to it. I'd like to plug some of those damn press leaks. It's impossible with this many people privy to all the information."

"I hear ya'."

About thirty-five minutes later, she went and got Rob. "Everything's all set."

Rob walked in and looked around. There were now eight people at the table. He looked at Beth and said, "I meant counting me,"

Beth rolled her eyes.

Rob Jamison, the new ASAC, was introduced to those he hadn't met, then said, "Lay out what we know, so far. But we don't have to go over that missing clue fiasco."

Beth signaled Mark Siene, who was back from Canada, to start. Mark said, "We were able to get a wealth of information from the interrogation of Kasra Khatani. He was our shooter in Toronto."

Rob interrupted, "He just gave it up?"

"Well not at first . . . until we showed him the newspaper article saying that two Saudi princes who were race fans were also killed in the attack. The Canadians threatened to deport him to Saudi Arabia. He couldn't talk fast enough, after that."

"Go on," said Rob

"Khatani claimed that Ali Naderi had some how found out what his sons Nouri and Sami were planning and approached Farid and Reza's father, Aram Danesh. Aram and Ali then confronted Kasra Khatani to see if he had anything to do with the plot. According to Khatani, Ali Naderi showed him a detailed plan for carrying out an attack on the Daytona Speedway. He told the two fathers that he had nothing to do with it and asked if he could have the written plan. He was surprised when Naderi gave it to him."

"When was this?" asked Rob.

"Early January," Mark answered.

"OK, go on."

"He claims he then gave it to his handler and didn't hear anything for a week or so."

"Did he name his handler?" asked Rob.

"Yeah, the Canadians are still looking for him. He's disappeared, but we think he may have been the second terrorist in Daytona."

"OK . . . ?"

"Then he said he was told that they were going ahead with the attack, but would be using their own men who would be on the scene. They gave Khatani instructions on what he had to do. He said not much happened on his end until he had to do the killings."

"Do we know how Ali Naderi got hold of his son's plan?"

Mark explained about the Canadian authorities finding out how Nouri's father was spying on the boys. The father destroyed Nouri's laptop computer but hadn't got around to erasing the files that he downloaded from the back-up site to his own computer. The Canadians had all Nouri's files for the last six months. He encrypted the files, but they said they got help from one of our intelligence agencies in decoding them.

"Did they say who helped them on our side?"

"The people I was working with didn't know," answered Mark. "Once we had the plan, then we knew what happened."

Beth added, "We confirmed much of it. There's a report of a stolen tanker truck in the vicinity, and an employee in a nearby high-rise hotel overlooking the Daytona Speedway was shooting some video that day. We analyzed it and saw the fuel truck enter the grounds and then blow-up."

Mark went on, "Khatani says that after he killed the men in the garage, he used Nouri's cell phone to give the terrorists a coded message and Sami Naderi's phone number."

"Sami Naderi was the brother we weren't watching?"

"Yes," said Beth.

"Do we have any idea who the driver of the truck was?"

"The Israelis helped us with that," said an agent who had just returned from Tampa. "This is what we are able to surmise, some of it's conjecture, but it all fits. The Tampa police got a call on a shooting. The victim turned out to be Sami Naderi. We know from Nouri's plan that the younger brother was to purchase the supplies and then meet the others," said the agent, talking a little too fast.

"We think the terrorists met Sami, gave him some story about the brothers not being able to make it, got the stuff and then shot him."

"Do we know how these assholes got into the country?" asked Rob.

"Not yet," said Beth.

"Okay, then what happened?"

"This is where it gets a little fuzzy. Somehow, the terrorists stole a truck full of gasoline from a fuel company in Tampa. They killed a yard worker. We're waiting for a ballistics report to see if they used the same weapon to kill Sami Naderi. We also found an abandoned SUV stolen from a rental car company in Buffalo. If they followed the plan that Naderi put together, they would have mixed the fuel with liquid oxygen and the hydrogen peroxide. They probably did this before leaving the fuel terminal."

"Do we know how they set off the bomb?"

"The Naderi plan didn't say much about that."

"Do we know how they got hold of the liquid oxygen and the peroxide?"

"We're thinking that Sami Naderi purchased it, but we don't have any credit card record of the purchase."

"I'm having a problem with this—I just can't see how one gasoline truck could do so much damage," said Rob.

"We talked to a military weapons expert and he said that the way the truck blew was maybe a one in a thousand shot. They're trying to simulate the explosion again on a much smaller scale, of course, but so far they haven't been able to," said one of the other special agents.

"Okay, so what else don't we know?" asked Rob.

"We don't know who else saw Naderi's plan after Kasra Khatani gave it to his handler. We don't know who arranged to have the Hezbollah terrorists come to the United States, how they were financed and how they got into the country. But it's safe to assume that it wasn't over the Mexican border because of where the SUV was stolen. There were plenty of fingerprints left and we sent them to Interpol."

"That's a lot not to know. Is that it?"

"Yes, so far. Do you want a written summary of this meeting?" asked Beth.

"Yeah, I need to brief the SAC later on today. Do we have a plan to go forward in the investigation? Does everyone know what they have to do?" Rob looked around and everyone nodded, so he got up and left. "Unbelievable," he muttered to himself.

38

MAYOR MILTON FRYER was getting ready to accompany the unidentified remains to their final resting place in the Florida National Cemetery. The recovery workers had collected thousands of bone fragments and stored them in the Volusia county morgue awaiting burial. The actual recovery effort didn't begin until two days after the explosion. It took that long to rescue those individuals trapped in the debris and to get them the medical help they needed. Milton thought it would've taken longer if the Navy amphibious warfare ship, USS *Wasp* with its 26 helicopters hadn't just left port from Norfolk on its next deployment. The president had ordered the United States military to support the National Guard effort, and the *Wasp* was part of that support. The ship's captain had the vessel anchored two miles offshore Daytona Beach by 4:00 P.M. the following day. Its helicopters undoubtedly saved many lives. The medical personnel in the ship's hospital attended to 600 casualties, while the Marines helped the National Guard with recovery, logistics and security.

Milton remembered watching the recovery effort. There were National Guardsmen and Marines wearing dessert camouflage carrying children's beach toys. They were using the little shovels and sand sifters to search through the ashes for charred bone fragments and teeth. It was gruesome work, and many of the service people became ill. When their little pails were full they emptied them into five-gallon paint buckets, similar to the kind one would buy at a home improvement store. They then delivered the buckets of fragments and the larger body parts to a makeshift morgue in the Ocean Center. The Army Corp of Engineers had enhanced the building's air conditioning system to keep the bodies cold while medical examiners from all over the Southeast worked to identify the dead. It was the pieces that the medical examiners couldn't identify that Milton Fryer would be accompanying to the cemetery today.

It was known that many of the missing were veterans and their spouses. They were entitled to a spot in any National Cemetery in the country, including Arlington National in Washington, D.C. Since it was impossible to separate the veterans from those others who were killed and not identified, the president of the United States had ordered that they all be buried together.

He commissioned a mausoleum similar to that of Arlington's Tomb of the Unknown Soldier, to be built at the Florida National Cemetery in Bushnell. Since most of the victims where from the southeastern region of the country, it made sense to the president to construct the memorial closer to their family's homes. An army of stonemasons, many of whom were volunteers, managed to build in two weeks a beautiful marble structure that would hold the remains. They would construct a visitor's center later on, Milton was told.

As he readied himself, he thought about what had transpired in the last three weeks in his city. He was proud of the way all the city leaders had come together and brought the city back to some sort of normality, as if that was even possible. Once they had completed the rescue and recovery effort in the first weeks, the Mayor had met with the city commissioners, or at least the ones not killed, to discuss how to carry on the city's business. Daytona Bike Week would be coming up and they discussed whether to ask the motorcyclists to stay away. The races at the Speedway would, of course, be cancelled, but there were hundreds of other events that could still take place. In the end, the commissioners decided to let the bikers come down because businesses depended on their twice-yearly visits, and jobs would be lost in the area if the event was cancelled. They didn't think many motorcyclists would come, anyway. Milton thought about how wrong they'd been. The motorcycle community came in numbers never before seen. They said they wanted to pay their respects.

Overall, motorcycle riders were a very patriotic lot. It was Sunday, the last day of Bike Week, and many riders would be accompanying the funeral procession the 110 miles to the Florida National Cemetery in Bushnell, which was located just east of I-75, on the opposite side of the state. Milton knew that a motorcycle group called the Patriot Guard Riders, of which he was a member, was organizing the ride. This group was founded years earlier to protect family members from a fundamentalist Christian group that was protesting against gays at military funerals. The Patriot Guard Riders, over the years, had morphed into an honor guard for all fallen heroes and veterans. They usually lined themselves up in long rows exhibiting the Stars & Stripes and rode along with funeral cortège if they were asked. Today they would be doing the same thing, but Milton heard from the organizers that they expected many other riders were also to accompany them. When the Florida State Patrol heard this, they did a smart thing. They had radio stations broadcast that they would be closing the normal passing lanes of I-4, the Florida Turnpike and I-75 to all traffic not part of the funeral procession along the entire route. In this way, other drivers could take their exits without interfering with the funeral line. The governor also suspended toll collecting on all state roads for the day.

The motorcyclists would be assembling on the old Speedway grounds—now completely cleared. The city had what was left of the structure demolished and all the burned out cars removed. Now all that remained was a scarred parking lot and a field full of flower bouquets mourners had been leaving for the last several weeks.

It was Sunday morning and the cable news networks were covering the event live from helicopters. What the viewers saw tore at their heartstrings. Police cars, representing every state in the union including Alaska and Hawaii, led six black funeral cars, each holding the unknown remains in military style metal caskets draped with American flags. A number of limousines followed, carrying Milton and the other dignitaries.

Following them were the motorcyclists who, while waiting, had begun to pick up the flower bouquets and tie them to their bikes. A rumor had spread through the crowd of leather-clad riders that the city would be removing the flower offerings the next day, anyway. The crowd decided, in that case, they should take the flowers to the cemetery. The motorcyclists formed up two to a lane in a staggered formation. Nobody could believe it; motorcycles covered the entire funeral route from Daytona to Bushnell—all 110 miles. The funeral procession had reached the cemetery, and some riders hadn't even left the Speedway parking lot. Many news reports put the figure at 120,000 riders.

People were standing by the side of the roads everywhere they could find a space. Many saluted or put their right hand over their hearts. They watched as the high-speed procession went by, flowers blossoms blowing from the motorcycles, first a few at a time, then in large swirls. Soon the air was as full as a confetti drop of brightly colored petals forming themselves into little tornados moving over the onlookers. Children were catching petals by the handfuls, throwing them back on the route only to be blown back to be picked up and thrown again.

Of course, there were the protesters. The motorcyclists promptly ran them off everywhere they were encountered. Free speech was suspended for the day.

39

FORMER MAYOR, now congressional representative, Milton Fryer, was watching the TV monitor waiting his turn to be interviewed. Since moving to Washington two months before, he was a regular on the cable news networks. He was doing ten or twelve shows a week, now. He heard someone on one network describe him as a media darling, which he found amusing. Others likened him to the former mayor of New York in the similar way they both handled their cities' great tragedies. Since he was a former pastor and an articulate speaker, the media anointed him as the de facto spokesperson for the Christian Right. Milton found this quite ironic for two reasons. If there was one group that disagreed with him most, it was the Christian Right. And the other was the fact that he had all but lost his faith during the last several months. However, that didn't stop him from using religious arguments to make his points.

Following the internment ceremonies, the Florida governor requested him to return to Daytona Beach in his limousine. During the journey, the governor asked Milton if he would like to be appointed to the United States Congress. The speedway attack killed the congressman for the Seventh District serving the Daytona Beach area, who had nearly a year to go in his term. The governor told Milton that he liked the way he had taken charge of the crisis and how deftly he handled the press. Milton was surprised at the offer to fill the remaining term since he wasn't even in the same political party. Milton found out later the governor was afraid that, with his new notoriety, he'd run against him in the next gubernatorial election. Now here he was—a national figure. The media frequently ran excerpts of his eulogy, considered by many to be one of the best speeches of the last 25 years. Milton was proud of that. He credited it to all the late nights he spent writing sermons as a former pastor.

As he waited for his interview, which would be in the second segment of the show, he wondered who would be his counterpoint that night. Lately, the shows' producers were pitting him against some real losers. He knew it was a media trick to find the worst spokesperson they could find to present the argument for the side the show's host didn't agree with. Except for one cable network, this usually meant the conservative was the show's goat. What puzzled Milton was that he was so far right in his views that a year ago they would have branded him a nut and not let him anywhere near their TV cameras. But Milton was popular with talk show producers because he got good ratings. He usually had more than one offer a day, and he normally chose the left-leaning shows. They were more fun and asked less pointed questions than their conservative counterparts, who went out of their way to appear fair and balanced.

Even his interview last Sunday on *60 Minutes* was full of softball questions that he easily parried. He dropped a number of bombshells during that interview that he supposed they would ask him about tonight. "Congressmen, you're on in seven, six, five, four . . ."

He was introduced by the host of the show along with a woman named Kelly something who represented a left wing spin-off organization from the American Civil Liberties Union. He had heard this woman speak before, and her views were so radical that she'd make him look like the moderate. He supposed he'd probably hit a few questions right out of the ballpark tonight.

The interviewer asked, "The other night on national television you stated that you didn't have much trouble with illegal immigration. Given your party's views on the issue, I find this somewhat surprising."

Milton answered, "Well, Keith, it's a fact that illegal immigration has put a strain on many government services and our healthcare system. This is especially true now since the tragic events in my hometown have posed a number of challenges for many of our citizens. However, most of these men and women who illegally crossed the border were from Mexico and South America. The government estimates that 25 million people came to our country this way—the vast majority being Christian, mostly Catholic, but Christian, nonetheless.

That equates to more than a thousand Christians for every Muslim that's come to our shores. Look at the problems they're having in Europe with the Muslim influx and what it's doing to their political systems."

"Are you saying that it's better to have Christians come to our country than Muslims?" asked the women from the liberal organization.

Milton looked directly into the camera and said, "Yes, I am."

There was dead air for about five seconds, while neither the host nor his women guest could think of anything to say to that. The shows director cut to a commercial.

When they came back, the women said to the host. "I can't take anything this man says seriously. He even advocates killing civilians as a means to stop terrorism. He said that the other night on another network."

"Would you like to respond to that?" the host said, thanking the women in his mind for being so provocative.

"I don't know if my friend Kelly here . . ."

"Don't call me your friend."

"I'm sorry. I forgot you don't have any friends. But let me continue. I never advocated anything. I just asked the question when exactly did we in the United States say that killing civilians was off limits. We have a long history of doing just that as a deterrent to keeping the other side from doing it to us. We had a policy called MAD, or mutual assured destruction, during the cold war that said to the Soviets, 'if you bomb our cities we will bomb yours.' I'm part Native American, and the

United States Army wiped out whole villages of Indians when settlers were attacked. During World War II, considered by many people the most just war ever fought on foreign soil, we routinely attacked population centers in response to the Germans who were doing the same. The Allies fire-bombed the city of Dresden, killing 35,000 civilians."

"But we live in a more enlightened age now."

"Enlightened age? Muslim terrorists killed 65,000 people in my city. And, they're going to do it again."

"Not all Muslims are bad."

"I never said that, did I? But let's do the math. Islam is the largest religion in the world. Over twenty percent of the world's population is now Muslim. That's more than 1.2 billion people. Let's say that only one percent want to hurt us . . ." Milton thought for a second. "Let me correct that. Let's just say 1/100 of one percent are capable of suicide attacks against us, that still leaves over 120,000 people. We can't defend against that."

Milton left them speechless for the second time that night, so they cut to commercial again. During the long break, the telephone switchboard lit up and the network was bombarded with e-mails. The feedback was running 20 to 1 in Milton's favor. The host was stunned. His demographic was one of the most liberal on cable television. Although Milton was scheduled for only two segments on the show, they asked him if he could stay for another half hour. He agreed. "Back in seven, six, five, four . . ."

"For those just joining us, we're live with Congressman Milton Fryer, as many of you know was the mayor of Daytona Beach during the tragedy several months ago. Congressman, although you denied Kelly's assertion that you are advocating violence against civilians, it would sound like that this is exactly what you are suggesting to many in our audience," the host said, thinking that not only does the audience think that, but they're agreeing with him.

Milton promptly answered, "Are you asking me if there is a viable strategy that includes targeting civilians? I believe there are several, but I'm not proposing that we do that at this point."

Kelly jumped on the last phrase. "What do you mean, at this point? It sure looks like you left the door open for this despicable act."

"Can you give us an example of one of these viable strategies?"

"Sure, Keith. Again, I'm not advocating we do any of these things. Let's look at the problem of suicide bombings, like what happened at the Speedway. The bastards were killed in the attack, so many people like Kelly here, think there's nothing we can do about it but set up a *dialog* with our enemies. Who really thinks that will work? These people hate us. Now, Kelly can sit around with all the other hand-wringers and hope it doesn't happen again, or we can do something about it."

"Can you be more specific? I think our audience would like to hear a plan since no one as yet has come up with a solution to people intent upon killing themselves in an attack."

"Keith, you're right, these people don't have a problem forfeiting their lives for some religious or political motive. But would they forfeit the lives of their families?" I mean if a suicide bomber knew that there would be severe retaliation against their families, would they be as likely to attack? I think not. If they knew their parents, siblings, cousins, friends would possibly be killed in retaliation, would they go through with it? Maybe some would, but most would not, at least not without asking permission," Milton said with a smile.

The host knew this was great television. People would be talking about this for weeks. They had one segment to go, and he figured Milton couldn't possibly say anything more controversial. The host was wrong. In the meantime, the network's website had crashed because of the number of hits it was getting.

"Back with Congressman Milton Fryer and Kelly Sampling of the Institute for World Dialog . . . Kelly, do you have a comment about what Congressman Fryer was saying?"

"You bet I do. That was the most outrageous thing I've ever heard. Nobody's going to go along with that."

"Like nobody's going to kill 65,000 of our citizens?" Milton shot back. "What's your solution, Kelly? Let them take over. It wouldn't be the first time in history that Muslims took over a Western country. Maybe you think we should surrender to them. Okay, let's do that. I'm a man. My life won't change that much. Sure, I'll have to pray five times a day and give up drinking alcohol, which is probably a good thing. Maybe I'll be required to grow a beard—not that big of a deal. I can still pray to my God in private. However, look what happens to women in some Muslim countries. You know it'll be the radicals, not the moderates that take us over. In other words, think of the Taliban and its persecution of women—no education, and little medical care, covered from head to foot. Any man would be allowed to beat a woman for the slightest infraction. Atrocities, like cutting a women's finger tips off for wearing nail polish, would be committed. Should I go on?"

The public reaction to Milton's comments was incredible. Polls taken by several organizations showed seventy percent of the American people thought he made sense. Another 51 percent thought the United States should employ some of the methods Milton described. Milton's popularity on the talk circuit absolutely soared. Promos between commercials always included Milton's next scheduled appearances.

40

THE SPECIAL AGENT whose turn it was to drive this week, dropped Rob Jamison in front of his home. Rob hated car pooling and resisted it as long as he could, but with the gas lines still stretching for blocks, and the price of fuel now passing $9.00 per gallon, he didn't have much choice. He tried riding his Harley to work a few times—it did get over forty miles per gallon, but he was rained on every time. He didn't mind so much getting wet, but cleaning all that chrome was a real chore. Since Sheryl spent most of the day at home, it was her job to fuel the vehicles. She said she didn't mind because she used the time to study for the Florida Bar Exam. That was her plan now since her career in law enforcement was over.

Rob walked into the house to find Sheryl standing barefoot in the kitchen chopping vegetables. She looked good standing there with just a bikini top and a pair of little white shorts. To Rob's surprise, Sheryl had become a gym rat and spent at least two hours a day at a local health club, which was within walking distance from where they lived. Walking in the sun, had given her a nice tan and with the ten pounds she lost, she was looking good. Sheryl was always attractive, but now she was turning heads. She stopped what she was doing, walked over and kissed him on the cheek. Even barefoot, she was at least an inch taller than his 5'8" frame. He remembered that when they worked together, she would always wear the biggest heels she could get away with, which he always thought was an attempt to intimidate her shorter comrades. Sheryl was full of surprises. He thought she was still shallow and manipulative, but she was interesting, also. She turned out to be a neatnik. Everything had to be arranged just so. At first this drove him crazy, but he quickly got used to someone picking up after him. He was amused because this neatness didn't extend to the master bath or their shared closet. Rob had moved his clothes to one of the other bedroom closets, and now used another bathroom. The master bath counter had at least fifty bottles, tubes and other beauty paraphernalia. He guessed it seemed to be working though.

"Are you making dinner?" The answer was obvious, but he knew that phasing it another way, like, "What's for dinner?" always got him a scowl.

"Uh hum. I thought I'd make us a nice salad with hearts of palm and artichokes."

"Where did you get the lettuce?" Rob asked, knowing that fresh produce was almost non-existent.

"Mr. Moretti."

Rob knew Sheryl had befriended the 80-year-old widower who was his next door neighbor. He had a large vegetable garden in his back yard. Lately, Sheryl spent a couple afternoons a week talking with him on his patio, keeping him company. Now Rob knew why.

"He also gave me some chicken that he had in his freezer. I thought you could put it on the gas grill."

"Can't do it. The propane bottle's empty and you can't buy it anywhere. Just one more thing that's being rationed"

"No problem, I can broil it."

Rob would normally have grabbed a beer, but there wasn't any alcohol in the house. Sheryl had given up drinking wine and Rob didn't want to do anything to cause her to start up again. He suspected that she had a problem in that area and it was probably a major cause of her screw-up.

"Why don't you put on the TV? Dinner will be ready in about an hour."

Rob went over and sat down on the couch, which acted like a room divider, separating the kitchen from the rest of the great room. He looked around and noticed that she had replaced his art on the walls with hers. He thought this woman's not going to change.

"Have you seen the remote?"

"It's probably under that magazine."

He looked down at the coffee table and there was a copy of Brides Magazine. He stared at it and mumbled to himself, "Not in this century—or the next."

"Did you say something?"

He didn't hear her walk up behind him. "What's with the Brides Magazine?"

"It was in our mailbox. It belongs to a neighbor up the street."

Rob thought, I'll bet, and picked up the magazine, sure that there wouldn't be an address label on the back. To his surprise there was. The mail carrier must have transposed the last two numbers with his own street address when delivering the mail. He thought he misjudged her when she said, "Rob, where's our relationship going?"

Then his cell phone rang. This was something that also annoyed him. He hated his new cell phone. When Sheryl left the FBI, she had to get a new phone and pay for it herself. She signed them both up for a family plan, getting two identical phones free with the one-year commitment. The manufacturer had evidently designed the phone for frequent text messaging, something Rob rarely, if ever, did. His phone had a full keypad and was complicated to use.

While he was on the call, Sheryl had gone back to making dinner. He figured he dodged a bullet for now. He had no idea where their relationship was going. As he looked around his house, it seemed obvious that Sheryl had some ideas on the subject, though.

During dinner, Sheryl told Rob the pool pump was making noise. While he was out looking at it, her cell phone rang. "Hello."

The person on the other end said, "Who's this?" Sheryl thought that was rude, so she said, "Who's this, and who are you looking for?" As she said it, she realized she had answered Rob's phone by mistake, and it was Beth on the other end.

"Sheryl, is that you?"

Just then, Rob walked back in and Sheryl handed him the phone. "It's Beth."

"Hello."

"What in the world is Sheryl doing answering your cell phone?"

"It's a long story. What do you need?"

"I wanted to tell you the meeting for tomorrow has been pushed back until the afternoon. No need to come in early. What's the deal with Sheryl?"

"I'll explain it tomorrow."

After he signed off, Rob went looking for Sheryl who was nowhere to be found. It's a good thing he thought; he wanted to kill her. He didn't relish the conversation he'd have to have with Beth the next day.

Rob put the TV back on and started flipping channels. It was summer so everything seemed to be a rerun. Rob thought 500 channels and nothing on. Sheryl loved the reality shows. Rob hated them. The cable news shows weren't much better. It seemed every time the FBI discovered something new involving the Speedway attack, it showed up on cable in a matter of hours. Rob tried to plug the leaks and even had everyone in the Jacksonville office, except the SAC, take lie detector tests to find out who was talking to the press. He reckoned that the information was coming from one of the higher ups.

Sheryl returned home carrying a bag. From the way she was holding it, Rob could tell it contained a skinny bottle. He knew exactly what it was.

Sheryl said, "Are you mad at me?"

Of course he was mad at her, but he had to make a decision. So he said, "No, I'm not mad," as he got up, took the wine bottle from the bag, opened the French doors and tossed the bottle into the pool. "You don't need that." He sat down on the couch, and she came and sat next to him. "I'm sorry," she said.

In a few minutes, everything was back to normal. They were squabbling over the remote. He stopped on a cable news show and she said, "The news is just so depressing."

Rob thought everybody says that, but it really was depressing. They were watching a clip of the unsuccessful presidential candidate talking about the current president. It had been a bitter election and after over a year there was still some bad blood between the former rivals.

"He promised you all that he would protect you. Did that happen? No, it did not."

The moderator asked, "Are you calling for his impeachment like some in your party?"

"I think it's too early for that, but I can understand the frustration of the American people. We know who's behind this, don't we? But the American people need more answers. I believe that, at the least, there should be congressional hearings. The administration should also appoint a special prosecutor to look into the matter. I don't have much faith in the attorney general to find out if there was any malfeasance in the administration, which contributed to our government failing us."

"So it's your feeling that the administration dropped the ball?"

"Absolutely—from what's come out so far, we had ample opportunity to stop this slaughter of our people, and they didn't do it. All we see now is the administration trying to cover their collective asses."

Rob, watching this, knew first hand who the politician was talking about. There was definitely an opportunity to prevent the attack and there appeared to be an Iranian connection. But so far it hadn't been proved. The story did leak that the FBI was looking into this connection.

Sheryl snatched the remote and clicked to another channel. They were interviewing Milton Fryer. "Hey, did I tell you I know him?"

"Yes, Sheryl, every time you see him."

"He liked me, you know."

Rob doubted that. Milton was on almost every night. The media seemed to love this guy. Rob thought he was outrageous and always rooted for the other guy during the discourse. Tonight Milton was talking about Israel, Russia and Iran. The foreign policy pundits had been speculating for weeks about Russia's response if the United States military attacked Iran. Rob heard some well thought out arguments on both sides, but what he was hearing now from Milton Fryer was so stupid he thought nobody could believe it. However, Rob knew how much easier it was to get people to believe a lie than the truth. He based this opinion on some of the cases of fraud he investigated working with the FBI. Obviously, good old Milton was also aware of this notion.

"So, Congressman Fryer, you're saying that Russia will never back Iran in a confrontation with us because of a secret alliance with Israel?"

"That's exactly what I'm saying."

Tonight, Milton's opponent was some hack with the worst hairpiece that Rob had ever seen. He lost all credibility before he opened his mouth, but he tried anyway. "The Congressman has absolutely no basis for that. There is a long history of antipathy between Israel and Russia."

Milton smiled and said, "Not so, the Soviet Union and now the Russians have been in bed with the Israelis since the early 1960s when they sold Israel fuel for atomic weapons."

The director had the cameras pan each member of the panel including the host. The look of incredulity appeared without exception. "What?" The guy with the bad hair said.

Rob thought that not even Milton would get away with that statement. He watched as Milton Fryer said, "I see you're skeptical, so let me share something I learned recently. In the late 1950s, Israel was right to be worried about an Arab invasion. In spite of the assurances given by the United States, its leaders didn't trust America to come to its aid. They knew that only the threat of an atomic bomb would keep their enemies at bay. Obviously they were wrong about that, but it has had a deterrent effect, nonetheless."

The host interjected, "Everyone knows Israel has atomic weapons. That's not in dispute."

"Actually, to this day Israel has never admitted to possessing them. They don't deny it, but confirming it would cause questions to be asked about how they developed them."

"They got the secrets from us. Remember the spy case in the eighties."

"That's correct," continued the congressman. "They did steal secrets from us about advanced nuclear weapons, but knowing how to build them is quite different from actually building them. Look at Iran and other countries, and the difficulties they're having in processing weapons grade uranium or putting their hands on plutonium."

"Your argument is ridiculous. There are numerous countries besides Russia and the United States that have developed their own nuclear weapons in the past."

"Name some," said Milton.

"China, India, Pakistan, North Korea," his opponent said smugly.

"What do China, India and Pakistan have in common?" Milton answered his own question. "They are all large countries with remote areas to hide secret facilities. In the case of North Korea, it is a closed society where nobody knows what's happening there. Have you ever been to Israel? It's tiny by comparison; it's the size of New Jersey. All of a sudden one day they come up with a bunch of nuclear weapons and nobody seems to know where they were developed."

"But why on earth would the Soviets want to sell

uranium or plutonium to Israel? The Arabs were their allies. Wouldn't they sell it to them first?"

"Remember, Jim, at the time Syria, Jordan, Egypt and most of the other Middle Eastern countries were relatively poor compared to Israel. They barely had enough money to buy conventional weapons from the Soviets."

"I still don't see why the Soviets would have sold Israel the weapons."

"The Soviet Union, besides their expensive military build up to counter us, also had huge outlays for their space program. They couldn't afford both. Israel would spend the money to develop the nuclear fuel anyway, so it was just as easy for them to buy the materials from the Soviets. And, I suppose a few people in the Kremlin got rich, also."

Rob was fascinated with Milton Fryer. As dubious as the story was, he knew that a large number of people would believe it. After all, Milton was a former preacher. However, a year ago the media would have dismissed him as an outright religious right-wing nutcase. Rob couldn't stand it any more, so he wrestled the remote away from Sheryl. He started channel surfing with Sheryl chirping at him, "Stop there . . . stop there!"

He recalled a comic talking about how the person who has the remote never finds anything interesting and the person who doesn't have the remote finds everything interesting. He thought how true that is. After cycling through the entire channel line-up, he settled back on CNN. There was a reporter talking about the day's speech from the chief commander of the new Iranian Ruling Council. CNN actually had a reporter who spoke Farsi, so she was translating from a notebook she had in her hand.

"Let me see here . . . the Iranian president called for a Muslim day of unity, a call to arms against the 'Great Satan' and Israel. He said the American imperialists are powerless and our brave freedom fighters can attack with impunity. He also told them to stop hiding their faces, to stand up and be counted. He then invited them to a rally to be held on July 4th in Tehran. I have to say it was truly shocking."

"He actually said those things?"

"Yes he did."

"Doesn't he expect reprisals by the United States?"

"Let me see here . . . in his remarks he also warned Washington, 'Iran will not fold as easy as Iraq'."

"Anything else?"

"Yes, he said that the Western media would not be allowed to cover the event and must be out of the country by July 2nd."

Rob, watching this, thought that the Iranians must be nuts. The American people already suspected that they had some involvement in the Speedway massacre. His remarks all but confirmed their belligerence. It almost sounded like he was declaring war on the United States.

Expecting to hear more, the conversation changed to a sex scandal involving some New England governor and a lobbyist. He guessed some things would never change. It wasn't very interesting, so he went over to the *fair and balanced* network. He listened for a while and must have heard the word *crisis* nineteen or twenty times. They were talking about the acute fuel shortage.

Rob thought *crisis* was probably appropriate. The latest was a South American dictator threatening to cut off oil supplies to the United States. He called the United States impotent. The commentators were speculating on the effect that would have on the American people as well as the economy. Rob had enough so he handed the remote to Sheryl, who settled on some inane reality show. Rob got up, went out to the garage and started polishing chrome on his motorcycle.

41

S PECIAL AGENT MARK SIENE wondered where
Beth Cuddy, his partner, had gone. Mark was excited. He had spent the last two months pouring over
thousands of financial records, and he had found some
interesting things. Mark was anxious to show someone,
and of course, his partner should be the first to hear
what he had found. Mark got up to stretch his legs and
asked another special agent who was walking by his
cubicle, "Have you seen Beth Cuddy?"

"She's in with the ASAC."

Mark knew that Rob Jamison and Beth Cuddy had
been partners and were close. They seem to like each
other very much. He thought Beth probably wouldn't
mind him briefing her and the ASAC at the same time,
so he started in that direction. The door was closed, but
the blinds were open. He was about to knock when he
heard Beth shout, "Rob, have you lost your mind?"
Mark thought Beth sounded quite angry. What Mark

didn't know was that Rob had come clean about his relationship with Sheryl. Mark couldn't help himself, and he loitered at the doorway.

"Rob, for God's sake, Sheryl . . .? Are you out of your mind? I thought you despised her. How long has this been going on?"

Mark didn't hear Rob's response, but he heard Beth repeat it. "Three effing years—you've been living with her for three years?"

"No, no. I told you Sheryl moved in after she sold her condo in February."

"What could you possibly see in that woman?"

Mark saw Rob notice him at the doorway. Rob Jamison waved him in. Mark could tell that Beth was annoyed at the intrusion, but Rob continued to wave him into the office, and asked, "What can I do for you, Special Agent?"

"I can see you're involved in something. I can come back." It was obvious Beth hadn't completed her business with Rob, but he could also see that Rob looked very relieved that he had interrupted their conversation. Mark was surprised when Beth ignored him and tore into her old partner again.

"I thought I was crazy. Months after she left here, I could still smell her perfume. It was on your clothes."

"Beth, maybe we should do this another time," Rob said, clearly embarrassed."

"You know, Rob . . ."

"Beth, that's enough! What did you need, Mark?"

Mark hesitated, wishing he had been more patient and had waited until Beth returned to their shared cubicle. He hesitated before saying, "I wanted to show you both what I found in my investigation of suspicious stock trades before and after the Speedway event."

"Sit down, sit down," said Rob.

After Mark had finished telling the ASAC and his partner what he had found, they seemed to forget all about their argument.

"Mark, this is big. We need to keep this real close. Have you told anybody else?" asked Rob, clearly worried about more leaks. "This can't get out."

Mark knew that the whole Jacksonville office was aware of the ASAC's antipathy toward the press, so he wasn't surprised at his cautionary instruction.

"This is what I'm goin' to do," said Rob. "I'll arrange a meeting with everyone on a *need to know basis* at the Hoover Building in D.C. Prepare for a formal presentation. I don't know yet how many will attend, but the fewer the better. This is really good work, Mark."

Two days later Mark was in Washington, D.C., accompanied by Rob and Beth. He spent most of the night putting the final touches on his PowerPoint presentation. He spent hours going over the data and he believed he had the proverbial *smoking gun*. Mark worked hard, trying to make his presentation as simple as possible. There would be people in the room who had no formal financial education. Mark also expected some big bosses would attend, since he was doing his presentation at the Hoover Building. He knew there was no room for anything other than a stellar presentation.

Mark joined the Bureau six years ago, after receiving an accounting degree from Wharton. He grew up in the

Fox Point section of Providence, Rhode Island, the son of an African-American father who had been with that city's police force for the past thirty years. His mother was a first generation immigrant from the Azores. Mark figured he was probably the only African-American in the FBI who could speak fluent Portuguese, a skill he hadn't yet used in the FBI. The skill he had used successfully was his propensity toward numbers and statistics. Growing up, while all his friends were avid basketball and football fans, Mark gravitated toward baseball, which many described as a game of numbers. He could recite statistics for every Boston Red Sox player who was ever on the team. Mark was a good athlete in his own right. In his teens, he was a star player for the Hope High School baseball team, but he realized he'd never be good enough to play in the majors. Mark liked the idea of being a police officer like his father, but he also thought about accounting as a career. He was torn, which had made it difficult for him as a senior when applying to colleges. One day, while he was explaining his dilemma to his guidance counselor, she suggested the FBI. She explained the Bureau liked to hire people with Law or Accounting degrees. Mark made up his mind right then as to what he wanted to do for an occupation. So eleven years later here he was—ready to make the biggest presentation of his career, and he was determined to make a good impression.

The group was filing into the big conference room that was used for large meetings at the FBI. Mark was surprised to see the Attorney General of the United

States walk in with the FBI Director. He was thankful that he had made the extra effort in his preparation. When the group had finally settled down, Mark began his oration, although not before dropping his laser pointer; he was nervous.

"I'll try to make this as clear as possible for those of you unfamiliar with the stock market and how it works. So, forgive me for over-simplifying some concepts, if you do happen to be among the initiated," Mark began stiffly.

"In the stock market, for every buyer there has to be a seller. If I think the stock is going up, I have to find someone who thinks the stock will go down. The stock exchange and brokerage houses simplify this process, so it's automatic. Computers match up buyers with sellers."

"Now, what happens if I'm absolutely positive a stock will go down, but I don't own it? Some of you, at this point, would think that's a good thing. However, there are people in the market who know how to take advantage of this situation and make money." Mark showed a PowerPoint slide with a bunch of numbers. He pointed to the slide projected on the screen with his laser pointer. So far, he still had their attention, so he relaxed a little. He continued.

"There's a transaction called a *short sale* or selling short. Let me give you a scenario. A trader borrows a hundred shares of a stock that is currently selling for $10.00 a share from his brokerage house and immediately sells them for $1,000. So far he hasn't put out any money. A few days later the stock goes down to $8.00 a share. He buys one hundred shares at the new price, which costs him $800, to replace what he borrowed. This is called *covering a position*. When everything is settled he made $200 without taking any money out of his pocket," explained Mark, hoping someone would ask the obvious question. Bingo, here it comes. One of the bosses raised her hand and asked, "What happens if the stock goes up instead of down?"

Mark clicked to the next slide. "If the stock continued to rise, the trader would get pressure from the broker- age house to cover his position at the current price. This is why this type of trading is so speculative. You'd have to really believe the stock price is going to fall or you would never make a trade like this," said Mark.

Many heads were nodding in the audience, so he continued without asking for any questions. "After the 9/11 attack back in 2001, the whole market was battered for a time, but some stocks took more of a beating than others—mainly anything to do with the airlines or tourism. What we've been doing over the past several months is looking for short sales on the Friday before the Daytona attack, maybe pointing to people who had prior knowledge of the event, which would most certainly push these stocks down again." Mark looked around the room. He knew what they were waiting for, but they were in for a surprise.

"What we found was there was no unusual trading of these stocks, especially short sales," Mark was ex- pecting the buzz in the room, and he got it. He actually heard someone say, "Then, what are we here for?"

Mark quieted the room down by saying, "Now wait a minute . . . what we did find was that there were short sales, but they were completely random. At first, we were disappointed like all of you, but then we realized this would never happen in reality. It was too random, as if a computer picked the stocks for the short sales. Remember, someone has to feel sure that a stock will go down before they'll sell short. By the way, this is a good way to catch insider trading scams," he started to digress then he brought himself back.

"Someone or some group had to know the whole market would go down on Friday before the attack," Mark stopped to emphasize the point.

"Doesn't the whole market go up and down on a daily basis, anyway?" asked the attorney general.

"Not exactly," answered Mark. "What you hear reported in the news are averages going up and down. For example, you hear the 'Down Jones Industrial Average went up fifteen points' or whatever. It's a rare event when the price of almost every stock in the market falls. Certainly, you'd need these conditions if you're going to short sell randomly."

There was a loud buzz in the room. Mark looked over at Beth, who was smiling at him. Now he was completely relaxed and clicked the next slide in the PowerPoint presentation. It showed a number of boxes with company names and arrows going this way and that way, up and down, circling around. "When we tried to trace the short seller this is what we found," Mark clicked again. "However, when we followed the money, we found this: the transactions were made through 87 different brokerage accounts, all owned by seven members of the new Iranian Ruling Council."

Mark heard the words he was looking for—*the smoking gun.*

"Do we have any other evidence? Did anything happen with the derivatives?" asked Mark's old boss.

Mark looked around and knew half the audience didn't have a clue what a derivative was, so he tried to explain it. "For those of you unfamiliar with derivatives, they are things like stock options, where you can purchase the right to buy or sell a stock at a specified price. So if I felt strongly that a stock would go down, I could purchase the right to make you buy it at a higher price. This is called a *put option* or putting it to someone. This isn't as speculative as selling short, but you do have to pay for *puts* when you purchase them. Therefore, the money must be in your account. We saw no evidence of anything strange going on with derivatives probably because our friends didn't have the money to buy them or it was too risky to move a large amount of cash around. As you know, we've made it difficult for people to move large sums of cash because of the reporting requirements."

The group asked a few more questions and the FBI Director adjourned the meeting, but not before admonishing them that everything they heard would not be discussed with the press. He told them he would use lie detectors if there were any leaks.

On the way out of the room the attorney general said to the director, "Thank you for the briefing. This can't get out. I want all this information verified. This is explosive stuff. I'm not going to the president with this until we're sure this information is correct. Also, we have to find at least one more link to this Iranian cabal."

The director said, "I agree, Mr. Attorney General."

42

U NLIKE HIS PREDECESSOR, the current president of the United States was a news show junky.
Shortly after taking office a little over a year before, he
had six brand new high definition flat screen monitors
installed in the Cabinet Room. He would've put them in
the Oval Office, if the first lady hadn't called that tacky.
The Cabinet Room was located on the other side of his
secretary's office, so he didn't have far to go. Over the
last few months he frequently brought in his work and
sat at the long table, watching the different news shows.
This habit annoyed both his staff and the Secret Service.
Conference space in the West Wing was at a premium
and his staff could no longer schedule meetings there.
The Secret Service had gone tactical several times, hearing the president's shouts. When they burst in, guns at
the ready, they found the president yelling at the television.

As the president walked into the Cabinet Room this day, he found the secretary of Homeland Security arguing with his secretary of Energy. This was a frequent occurrence since the events in Daytona Beach.

"It was a stupid thing to do."

"You seemed all for it at the time, as I remember."

"I didn't know at the time, you were just covering your ass."

"That's a bunch of crap and you know it. There were legitimate reasons for that decision."

The two men acknowledged his presence by nodding, but then went right on arguing. In this case, the president had to side with his secretary of Energy. The decision by Homeland Security not to allow any fuel deliveries without a police escort was a disaster. It started a series of unintended consequences that had brought the country's economy to its knees.

"How was I supposed to know the locals didn't have their act together?"

"You're supposed to know. You're the head of Homeland Security. Remember, FEMA works for you. You coordinate the local and federal response to disasters, or is that someone else?"

The two men were startled when they heard the president shout, "Damn it." At first, they thought he was yelling at them, but realized he was looking at the TV. "Do you hear what that moron is saying?" They listened as a South American dictator, whose country supplied a large amount of oil, was threatening to shut off shipments to the United States. The dictator's remarks were in Spanish, but were being interpreted into English.

"The United States has plundered our resources, stole our land and treated us like servants for the last two hundred years. It's time they learn some respect, we will no longer sell our oil to the Yankee imperialist thieves."

"Is this guy serious? If he doesn't sell it to us, who will he sell it to?" asked the secretary of Homeland Security."

"The Chinese will take all he has."

"Where would that leave us?" asked the president.

The Energy Secretary replied, "Up to now, the massive fuel shortages have been a distribution problem caused by our *friend's* bad judgment."

Before Homeland Secretary could fire back, the president said, "I've had enough of this finger pointing bullshit. Get on with it."

The Energy Secretary knew that the president was already angry, and not wanting to antagonize him further, he began his explanation in a monotone voice.

"Currently, we have severe gasoline shortages in the whole country with the exception of New Jersey, Texas and Louisiana. The same is true for low sulfur diesel. As you know, those states have most of the refining capacity. The price of regular unleaded will probably pass the $12.00 mark by the end of next month. There are long lines at gas stations and truck stops. Many stations have cut back on their operating hours."

"If it's a distribution and not a supply problem, why is the price going up so rapidly?"

"Your chief economist can probably answer that question better than I, but even though it's an artificial shortage caused by . . ." The president glared at him. "By internal policies, it's pushing the price of crude up on the world market to approximately $300 a barrel."

"What can we expect if that idiot goes through with his threat?"

"That would be a major disaster for our economy. Besides making the problems we are having now with factories closing for lack of parts, food shortages and people not being able to get to their jobs, we would face other extreme hardships. Many of our power plants run on fuel oil, so we could expect blackouts in certain areas of the county. Also, next winter many people in the northern states who still heat their homes with oil will have to find shelter elsewhere. Of course, air travel would be affected and . . ."

"Is that the worst case scenario?"

"No, Mr. President. Look around this room and notice how many things are made of plastic. Most Americans don't know that almost all plastics are made from petroleum. We use about 600,000 barrels a day to make it. Other than cans, we use plastic for the majority of food packaging. Plastic accounts for a large portion of medical supplies and equipment, as well as military hardware. The average American probably encounters plastic hundreds of times a day. A severe shortage will cause problems for us at least ten times more severe than the hardships that we've seen over the last several months."

This was grim news for the president. "At what point do you foresee this happening?"

"If our oil supply drops below 70 percent of our current levels, excluding distribution problems, we will begin seeing the effects."

The Homeland Security secretary, not wanting to be left out of the conversation added, "So the only people that wouldn't be greatly affected would be the Amish."

"Not true. They use candles, and candles are made from paraffin, which is a by-product of petroleum."

The president thought much of what he had just heard from his secretary of Energy was new to him. He suspected there was a lot more information he needed to know to handle this crisis effectively. There were probably members of his administration who were not being as candid as they should, thinking that he'd shoot the messenger. He believed the situation, as bad as it was in the United States, could get even worse without some strong measures. He thought, this president is not going to let things spiral out of control.

The president walked over to his Chief of Staff's office, who was surprised by his visit. Usually, the president's personal secretary summoned his chief. "Yes, Mr. President."

"I need you to do something for me. I want you to arrange a series of meetings at Camp David for next weekend."

"Who do you want to attend?"

"I want my entire Cabinet, including the other members of the National Security Council, and yourself, of course."

"What's the agenda?"

"I want a no holds barred discussion of where we currently are in this mess, as well as a forecast of what to expect in the next six months. Schedule it so that I meet with no more than two or three department heads at a time. I think they will be more open that way than having one big Cabinet meeting."

"OK, I'll arrange it."

"And, tell them I don't want anymore finger pointing, back biting, ass covering or whatever."

"Yes, Mr. President."

The president looked at his watch. It was now after 7:00 o'clock. This was the time the president usually retired to his private residence if there wasn't a State Dinner scheduled. Tonight he decided to watch a few more cable news shows. The first lady, when she was home, wouldn't let him watch in the residence because of his emotional outbursts. He had on the four major cable news networks, the *BBC* and the English version of *Al Jezzara*. As usual, he was taking a beating on all of them.

The president had tuned in on his former rival hinting around about starting impeachment proceedings against him. The presidential campaign had started civil enough and then had degenerated into bitter, name calling assaults on both sides. The wounds hadn't quite healed when the Daytona Speedway attack took place. The president walked over to the doorway and saw that his personal secretary was still at her desk. He knew she wouldn't leave until he retired to the residence. He thought he should be more considerate. "Shirley, how long was I in office when that Daytona business happened?"

"Thirteen months or exactly 397 days, I believe, Mr. President."

"Thanks, why don't you go home. I'm fine here," the president said, marveling at her ability to come up with the most arcane facts. He never remembered a time when he asked her a question where she didn't have an answer.

The president went back in the Cabinet Room and thought it was such bad timing. If he had been in office less than a year, the public would probably have held his predecessor accountable for not protecting the country. They blamed him for everything else. The former chief executive had the lowest approval rating of any president until now. He held second place in that dubious honor this week, according to the latest polls. The sentiment was that the administration should have been prepared. They were right. He should have foreseen something like this, but the enormity of the tragedy was way beyond his reasoning.

The president turned up the volume when he saw that one network was interviewing that wacko from Daytona Beach. He was talking about killing civilians as a solution to terrorism. The president thought the media loves this guy. To the president, he reminded him of Charles Manson for some reason. He supposed Milton Fryer's views were popular because the public wanted revenge for the ungodly acts perpetrated by the terrorists. At least after the World Trade Center, there was the Taliban in Afghanistan to attack, which gave some measure of comfort to many Americans. The president thought that what made it worse now, besides the horrific death toll, was this attack affected the geography of the whole country. While the September 11th attack temporarily caused some problems in the financial markets, for the most part, the tragedy was contained within the New York and Washington D.C. areas. Once the national mourning was over, people in other parts of the country went back to business as usual. This tragedy was completely different. Everyday the Daytona Speedway events were causing more hardships for the American people and the outlook for the future was getting grim.

The president turned off the six monitors and left for the night.

43

THE PRESIDENT WAS OUTSIDE BY HIMSELF, enjoying the early morning sounds of Camp David. The day was clear and he had a nice view of the mountains. He had intended to meet with his National Security Council, but decided against it. It was comprised of too many people. Instead, he would try to keep the discussions more intimate and less guarded. He needed good advice. All he seemed to be hearing lately was faultfinding and ass covering. The president was tired of it. Behind him he heard voices and the rustling of grass. When he looked over his shoulder from his seat at the picnic table, he saw the secretaries of State, Defense, and Treasury coming toward him. The president wanted a world view of their situation before delving into the myriad of domestic problems the country was facing. There was coffee and Styrofoam cups on the table, so everyone helped themselves.

The secretary of State looked around. "Is the rest of the council coming? I haven't even seen the vice president. He wasn't at breakfast."

"I didn't invite him," said the president. "It's just you gentlemen for now. I want our discussions to be candid. Everything you say today will be off the record. We're out here with no hidden microphones," he said, thinking about past administrations recording conversations in the Oval Office. The president pointed to the secretary of State and said, "Bill, why don't you start by giving us the usual overview of the hot spots, but this time, give me your best guess of where we'll be in six to nine months."

"What continent would you like me to start with? We've got problems everywhere."

The president thought this was starting out badly — like all the other national security meetings he'd attended since the first one — so he stopped the secretary. "I changed my mind; just tell me where we'll be at this time next year and what, if anything, we should do if the news isn't good."

"Okay, this is different. In my opinion, a year from now it may be very ugly. America will have much less influence on what goes on in the world than anytime since the days preceding World War I. Our superpower status will be superfluous. Local leaders will emerge, which will have much more of an effect on their regions. I suspect their influence will be in direct proportion to their antagonism toward the United States. They will hold us up as everything that is wrong with the world and the cause of most of their problems. A case in point is that lunatic in South America with his threats to cut off our oil. He's becoming more popular than Castro in his heyday."

"You foresee other countries doing the same?" asked the president.

"In my opinion we will see North Korea, at the very least, restart its nuclear program. They may possibly even begin incursions into the south. South Korea will undoubtedly try to appease them, which, as we know, won't work. We could be involved in hostilities there. The only thing that keeps them in check right now is the Chinese. Knowing this, the Chinese will begin undermining our relationship with Taiwan. They will begin making serious threats against the Taiwanese, hoping to use North Korea as a bargaining chip to eventually have us withdraw our support. That will make an invasion of Taiwan more likely."

The secretary of the Treasury asked, "What is it with the Chinese obsession with Taiwan? I don't get that."

"Taiwan to the Chinese is like Cuba to the United States. Here's a small country just off their coast with a political system that's alien to theirs, which has been a national embarrassment for decades. Does that sound familiar?"

"You're right, it sounds like Cuba."

"China also has a demographic problem. One of the unintended consequences of their one child policy was a notable imbalance in the Chinese society of young males verses young females. In the Chinese culture, it's the oldest male who takes care of aging parents, so abortion of female babies was much more prevalent.

History shows that countries with an over-population of young single males have either culled the herd by making war on their neighbors, or had to deal with civil unrest in their own country. We know how the Chinese feel about the latter. So I believe they're spoiling for a fight with someone in order to make a sociological adjustment—to put it a nice way."

"It's a good thing that their economy is so intertwined with ours now."

"That's right."

"What about the Russians?"

"Here's where the dominos start to fall. The Russians may demand that we scale back NATO to the 1980's membership. With their newfound oil wealth, they will threaten a military build up similar to what we saw in the cold war. If they start, our choice will be to do as they ask with NATO or respond with a military build-up of our own.

"What else do you foresee?" asked the president, shaking his head.

"There will be more trouble in Africa, with ethnic violence reaching new levels. We can expect millions more to die from civil wars and starvation. Speaking of ethnic violence, the problems in the Balkans have not gone away. We can anticipate another rash of anti-Muslim hostility probably leading to bloodshed. The Serbs will calculate that the American people will not come to the aid of Muslims in the region because of the unpleasantness at Daytona and our experience in Iraq."

"What about the Middle East? That's the area that worries me the most."

"We will move closer to an all-out war there, starting with Israel and Lebanon. Those problems were never resolved, and Hezbollah is stronger than ever. However, by far the biggest threat comes from Iran. Since the former leaders of the Revolutionary Guards overthrew their government things are worse—if that can be believed."

"The coup was inevitable," said the president. "I'm told that the most radical elements in Iran, the Revolutionary Guards, were allowed to keep their own military forces of nearly 400,000 active and reserves. They even had their own navy."

"That's true. Also, our CIA analysts tell us that the potential strength was closer to 11,000,000 people, all under the command of the Revolutionary Guards senior commanders."

"Are the Grand Ayatollah and his loyalists still in Turkmenistan?"

"They've set-up a government-in-exile there, hoping that the Iranian people will rise up and force the new Iranian Ruling Council to open parliament again and bring them back."

"I don't see much chance of that happening, not unless they can come up with some overwhelming force. It's amazing, I didn't think the Iranian situation could get any worse, but here we are."

"If they can find a way to unite the Sunni and the Shiites, then we may be looking forward to World War III."

"How likely is that to happen?" asked the secretary of Defense."

"Nobody's been able to do it for over a thousand years."

"So it's not likely?"

"I wouldn't say that. A change in leadership or policy toward the United States in Saudi Arabia and Egypt could bring about at least a partial reconciliation with the two factions. Syria is already onboard with Iran. Most likely Iran will try to capitalize on a shared antipathy toward the United States. Remember the old cliché, *The enemy of my enemy is my friend.*"

"Why did you think all-out war? Why not the same old thing? Somebody attacks Israel and Israel responds. They have a cease fire for awhile until somebody attacks Israel again. The moderate Middle Eastern countries ride the fence talking anti-western for their clergy while remaining friendly with the United States as a market for their oil and their defense," said the president.

The Treasury secretary answered the president's question. "China and India, especially the Chinese with their rapid industrialization—have a huge need for petroleum. The same goes for India. If we never bought another drop of Middle Eastern oil, they could still sell everything they have. I don't even think the world price would drop significantly."

The secretary of State said, "The most likely scenario for war is a coalition of countries including Syria, Egypt and Lebanon, headed by Iran. When that happens, it is inevitable that a major attack will be made on Israel. The Iranians will lead the effort."

"That sounds risky for the Iranians. Wouldn't they be afraid of an Israeli nuclear strike in retaliation?"

"Not if they have their own nuclear weapons. Think of what the Iranians could gain. The country that wins a decisive victory against Israel will rule that part of the world for the next two hundred years. If Iran had a common border with Israel, I'm sure it would have already happened. All the Iranians need to be successful is access. A coalition like the one I talk about would give them that. It would be very troubling."

The president thought that his secretary of State had a real gift for understatement. "So we're forced into a war with Iran to protect our ally Israel."

"It's either that or abandon Israel."

The secretary of Defense spoke up. "This is what happens when we appear weak. By not responding to the Daytona attack we looked weak and impotent . . ."

That remark really angered the president. "Then tell me; what would you have had me do, pick a country to bomb at random?"

"Mr. President, if the secretary of State is correct and we see anything even close to what he's talking about, we will not be able to respond effectively. We cannot hold off the Russians with our military might if we are engaged in hostilities in the Balkans, the Middle East and the Korean Peninsula. That's putting aside whatever else we may have to deal with in South America from that maniac."

"So what are our options? You tell me what I should do."

The Defense secretary could tell that the president was clearly angry with him, and if there were more people around he probably wouldn't be as candid as he was now. "You asked about options. We don't have any options. The last administration left us with some real problems. We have to replace much of the equipment and munitions that we used in Afghanistan and Iraq. This is especially true with our National Guard. They didn't have the best stuff in the first place. We need a trillion dollars to bring us back to where we were before we invaded Iraq; never mind matching a military build up by the Russians.

The president looked at the secretary of Treasury.

"He's correct, Mr. President—give or take a hundred billion or so."

"With regard to our National Guard, recruitment is way down due to their experience with extended overseas tours. The Guard wasn't organized for this. Currently, over sixty percent of National Guard's personnel are on active duty, helping the police agencies protect fuel trucks, which, in my opinion, is stupid."

The president said, "Don't start with that. I'm dealing with it."

"You asked me to be candid, so here is my opinion. If we have to fight in Korea and the Middle East and keep the peace in the Balkans, we will lose in at least one of those places."

The president was stunned. "I don't believe it. Our military has always been able to fight a two-front war."

"That may have been true in the past, but unless you decide on the nuclear option, we could lose a conventional war on two fronts."

"So you talking about personnel as well as equipment then?"

"Yes, Mr. President. Besides the National Guard, our volunteer force would not be large enough to prevail."

"Are you suggesting reinstating the draft? Or is there another way to get enough volunteers to staff the guard and regular military?"

"Reinstating the draft is one option. I don't believe it would be too popular with the American people."

"What about additional recruitment for the volunteer force?"

"There is no way to attract enough recruits the way our volunteer force is structured. We've already relaxed our criteria. We allow some people with criminal records to join. We also have a large number of people who aren't U.S. citizens in our services."

The Treasury secretary asked, "What are we, ancient Rome? We pay others to fight our battles?"

"Actually we've been doing this for quite some time."

"So there is no way to attract enough recruits?"

"Actually there is one idea that our military leaders have floated. We could relax the restrictions on age. It's estimated that if we open up our services to people age 62 and under, we could attract over a million citizens."

"How practical is that, though?"

"Except for our Special Forces, many jobs don't require up close and personal contact with the enemy. For example, most people in the army and almost everyone in the navy are in support and not combat roles. We also have high tech weapons that don't require much stamina or strength. We are not in the age of heavy shields and broad swords anymore."

The president said, "Neither option is very appealing. Gentlemen, let me summarize what I think you're telling me. The secretary of State thinks we are looking at major hostilities and the secretary of Defense tells us we don't have the equipment and people to win. Is that correct?"

The group nodded. The president thanked them for their candor, but was upset. He knew the next group probably wouldn't make him feel any better. It was warm, so he decided to go inside. He told his chief of staff that he was ready for the next meeting.

44

THE PRESIDENT WALKED BACK to the Laurel Lodge and went directly to the conference room. The secretary of Transportation was waiting, already seated, but Energy and Homeland Security hadn't yet arrived. The president knew it would get intense. "Gerri, while we're here, why don't you give me an update."

"News isn't good, Mr. President. The fuel shortage—I mean the fuel problem—there isn't really a shortage, as you know. Nevertheless, the shortage is now interfering with all modes of transportation. We have hundreds of ships waiting offshore to unload because the docks are full with containers waiting for pickup. The same goes for rail. At last count, there were over two thousand boxcars sitting on sidings, also waiting to be unloaded. In the meantime, the large trucking companies have taken about twenty-five percent of their equipment out of service due to fuel problems. The shortage of diesel fuel is acute in most areas of the country. Three and four hour waits at truck stops is not that unusual."

The president heard loud voices and knew that must be Homeland Security and Energy arguing. He watched the men enter the room.

"I'm sorry, Mr. President. Are we late?"

"No, Gerri's updating me on our transportation situation. Go on, Gerri, finish what you're saying."

"Gasoline availability is spotty. In some areas there is plenty of fuel. In other areas, we see shortages and long lines. It appears that the further away from a refinery or port city, the worse the situation, which seems to make sense. Prices everywhere are very high. We are looking toward $9.50 a gallon as an average."

The Transportation secretary went on . . . "Infrastructure is suffering, also. Companies that use heavy equipment for road and bridge repair are finding it difficult to get the equipment onsite, as well as acquiring fuel to keep the vehicles running."

"If things stay the same in terms of fuel availability, where do you see us in six months, better or worse?" asked the president.

"Assuming we stick with this idiotic requirement that all fuel trucks must travel in conveys or with police escorts, it'll get worse."

"We're modifying our procedures everyday," said the Homeland Security secretary.

"So far, everything you've done to make it better has made it worse. We have National Guardsmen and police protecting empty trucks while full ones wait. The stupidity of this arrangement is beyond belief."

The president said, "Okay, I don't need this today." He looked at his Energy secretary. "Have we solved our home heating fuel problem?"

"Well, it's June, Mr. President. We'd be screwed if it were December."

"If we were to see the worst case scenario—Diaz in South America, cutting off our fuel supplies and Iran causing mischief in the Persian Gulf, where will we be nine months to a year out?"

"If I may," said Homeland Security. "It will be a disaster beyond anything seen since the Great Depression. We have computer models that predict food shortages everywhere in the country. As you know, we've already had food riots in some cities. Many trucking companies are refusing to go into poor areas because of hijackings. As the shortages spread, the violence will probably increase. Think of the problems that Katrina caused in Louisiana—which were localized for the most part—and project them to the rest of country. The local police will probably not be able to stop the looting and many stores will close. Currently, most supermarkets have curtailed their shopping hours. This has caused food lines in some places for many goods, especially meat, poultry and fresh produce. Fish, unless previously frozen, will soon be non-existent. These problems will be magnified by a factor of at least ten. We will also see the emergence of a black market economy in some areas as some people will have more access to foodstuffs than others—for example, low paying supermarket and discount stores who don't put limits on the amount of goods their employees can purchase. There have been many reports of employee hoarding. Working for a discount or grocery store has become one of the more coveted jobs."

The Transportation secretary added, "I have to agree with everything the Homeland secretary just said, although it may even be worse than he's predicting."

"Damn it!" said the president, who was now on his feet pacing the room. "Is there any good news? I'm to believe that our whole society will just fall apart because of an oil shortage."

"Not everything's bad, Mr. President," said the Energy secretary. "Our energy grid will probably continue to function. Much of our electricity is still produced from hydroelectric, coal and some nuclear. Barring any nuclear catastrophe, we should easily be able to meet the country's electrical needs."

"How could that be?" asked the Transportation secretary."

"As the economy slows down, so will the need for power. That's one thing. Also, most coal for power generation comes directly by rail from the mines to the power plants, so we haven't seen any disruption of supplies. At some point we may have to relax environmental standards as we start running out of low sulfur coal to keep those plants online."

"What else?"

"We have a huge untapped reserve of natural gas, which has always been underutilized in the United States. Much of it moves by pipeline with almost no interruptions recorded in the past."

The Homeland Security secretary, seeing his boss was pleased hearing good news, wanting to get into the act said, "The Post Office is also working well."

"What are you talking about?"

"I've been told that mail is moving as freely as it always has. There are no delays in letters and packages getting to the intended recipients. In fact, there is a big increase for mail order food. Some of the more wealthy Americans have been utilizing this resource extensively for the last few months. I've been told by your personal chef that most of the food used in the White House is now acquired by mail order."

"Are you kidding me? Some of our citizens are going hungry and we're eating fancy expensive mail order steaks?"

"The poor always suffer the most," said the Homeland secretary, without any emotion.

The president glared at him, but knew that he was right. There wasn't much suffering going on for the first family in the White House.

The Homeland secretary, seeing that his initial foray into *good news* was quite unsuccessful, tried again. "There are some other positive developments. We expected to see a huge backlash against illegal immigrants, which didn't materialize. We expected our citizens to attack undocumented residents for using scarce resources and taking away needed jobs. It just didn't happen. It is very puzzling."

The president thought it wasn't that puzzling. People are listening to Milton Fryer. Perhaps there is a lesson to be learned here from the congressman. Since it was late in the afternoon, the president said, "Why don't we pick this up tomorrow. I want to talk with Labor, Agriculture and Commerce before I ask for recommendations."

45

THE PRESIDENT WENT OUTSIDE. He wished he had a cigarette. Once a heavy smoker, he had quit at the first lady's urging. If there was ever a time he wanted one more, he couldn't remember. After walking a bit, the craving went away, and he returned inside. The staff had put out some refreshments, and his secretaries of Labor, Agriculture and Commerce were indulging. The president thought about the things his nitwit Homeland Security secretary had said about the poor and decided he'd forgo the snacks.

"Why don't we get started? And, for a change, let's begin with the good news," said the president.

The three other people in the room were silent.

"You're telling me there is no good news?"

"Mr. President, the unemployment numbers are way up mostly due to massive lay-offs in the auto industry. The building trades are suffering because all commercial projects are all but shut down, and you already know about the housing market," said the secretary of Labor.

"It's hard to believe that one terrorist attack followed by one bad decision could cause this much disruption to our economy. There must be something we can do in the short run to mitigate this disaster. What about our ethanol production?"

The Agriculture secretary answered, "So far most of the ethanol that's been produced has been a replacement for other gasoline additives that were environmentally damaging. As far as adding to our fuel supply or replacing shortages, it has a negligible effect. We would have to ramp up production by several thousand percent to see any impact."

"Is that possible?"

"Mr. President, under no circumstances would you want to do that," said the Commerce secretary, looking worried. In my opinion our ethanol program has been a disaster."

"How so?"

"First, it's been totally ineffective in lowering our dependence on foreign oil. It has not reduced prices, but has caused some unintended consequences. The secretary of Agriculture could probably tell you what affect it's had on the price of corn used for feed. Prices for meat, poultry and other goods have increased dramatically and haven't been offset by any decrease in gasoline prices. Ethenol manufacturing calls for incredible amounts of water needed by other farmers for irrigation. In addition, we're now exporting much less in farm products to other countries, which is weakening our dollar and having a negative effect on our balance of trade. More troubling to me, is that even without our domestic problems, much of the corn used to produce ethanol formerly went to poor countries to prevent starvation. We used to stock pile excess surplus farm production and then give it away as part of our foreign aid program.

"How come I've never heard this before?"

"It's not politically correct to bash ethanol production on both sides of the aisle. Farmers are making more money, and environmentalists are holding it out as a way to use fewer resources. The buzz word is renewable biofuels."

"So if I can summarize your position, you believe that ethanol has had no effect in reducing our dependency on fossil fuels. It has caused food prices to rise and is having an adverse effect on our economy as a whole?"

"Yes."

"I agree, Mr. President," said the Agriculture secretary. "As far as our domestic challenges go, ethanol is not the answer in the short run and probably will not help solve our long term energy problems either."

"We're stuck with oil," said the president, shaking his head.

"Mr. President, undoubtedly you've heard some of our more liberal friends talk about *no blood for oil.* Ironically, oil is the lifeblood of our economy. We either find more or use less," said the Labor secretary. In my opinion, we must deal severely with any country that interferes with our ability to maintain our flow of oil.

It's an act of war. That was the Japanese position before World War II, when we interfered with their ability to source oil and they attacked us at Pearl Harbor."

"I know where you're headed with this," said the president. "I'm not ready to entertain any suggestions now. I want to fact-find first. So far, my options seem limited, though."

The president looked at his watch. "I think this is a good time to break for the day. I'm having a quiet dinner with the first lady and my chief of staff. I trust you gentlemen will be able to fend for yourselves for the evening."

"Sure, Mr. President."

"Do me a favor; try not to let my Energy secretary kill our friend in Homeland Security."

"I don't know, Mr. President. That's a lot to ask."

46

ENJOYING THE COOLNESS of the late afternoon, the president told the staff he would like to eat outside. He wanted to inhale the mountain air as much as possible before he returned to the White House the next day. He told his staff to keep dinner simple. The president couldn't get it out of his mind that while they were eating like aristocrats there were other people in the country who had to resort to breaking windows and stealing to get food for their families. It reminded him of those photos of the leader in North Korea with the buttons on his tunic straining while his people starved.

The President wasn't hungry anyway. He wondered for the first time whether he really was up for the job. Age and experience do matter, he thought. If he knew what was to happen, he would have never run for president and would've stayed within those comfortable walls of the Senate.

He saw the first lady approaching him. If it wasn't for this woman, he didn't know what he would do. He valued her advice tremendously.

"How's it going," she asked. "You look worried."

"If you heard what I heard today, you'd look the same way," the president said, seeing his best friend and now chief of staff headed their way. The president thought how much he loved this guy. His friend was always positive, no matter what the news. There were many a day during some of the primaries when the only smile he saw was his friend's face.

The chief of staff knew what the participants told the president. After each meeting, he debriefed them. He was also aware that there would be no good options when the president asked for suggestions the next day.

"What do you think I should do about the fuel truck escort business?" the president asked after his chief sat down.

"Well, boss, except for Homeland Security, everyone else wants you to have him rescind the order."

"Don't you think he should have consulted me before starting that business, anyway?"

"Do you think you would have told him not to do it?"

"Probably not."

"Do you see any downside to stopping it?"

"Economically no, politically yes."

"How so?"

"Once you put in a restriction, and say it's for safety or security, it's almost impossible to remove it without causing some anxiety. We could put ten Sky Marshals on every airliner making it near impossible to hijack, but the public would have a real problem if we removed the screeners. The other political party would characterize the move as reckless. If you force Homeland Security to abandon their police escorts, and there is another fuel truck incident, there is a good chance that your opponents will step up its calls for impeachment. And, may even succeed."

"I see your point."

"How about quietly stopping the practice?" asked the first lady. "There are fewer Sky Marshals on aircraft than there used to be, and I haven't heard any public outcry."

"For the most part, the Sky Marshals are anonymous. But those escorting the fuel trucks are in full uniform. It would be hard for the general public not to notice."

The president asked his wife, "What would you do?"

"Force Homeland Security to admit to the public it was a bad idea, and make those who want it to stay, defend it as a good idea."

The chief of staff said, "Boss, it would really improve moral around the White House to watch the secretary of Homeland Security fall on his sword."

"Do you think we could get him to do it?"

"There is a little matter with a cute young lobbyist," said the first lady.

"Boy or girl?" asked the president.

"Boy."

"That'll work," the president said, while looking at his chief of staff.

"You're going to make me do it?"

"No, get the attorney general to make some subtle inquiries while you give our secretary of Homeland Security a friendly heads-up."

"On another subject—the secretary of Defense told me that you got pissed at him."

"He's right, I did get mad. Everyone tells me that the United States looks weak. I hear it on the news. I hear it from the opposition. But, damn it, do I have to hear it from my own cabinet?"

"Because you don't want to hear it, doesn't mean they're wrong," said the first lady.

"You too? I asked the Defense secretary if he wanted me to pick a country to bomb at random . . ."

"Which country did you pick?" she said with a smile. "You know there really is some truth to what they're saying. It's one thing to call us names. It's quite another to hurt us economically. Forgive me, but aren't most wars fought over money, unless of course, it's religious zealotry."

"Okay, you pick a country," said the president.

"How about Venezuela or Iran?"

The president, thinking his wife was serious, said, "Venezuela is out of the question. But I don't need much of an excuse to let loose on Iran. Are they still going ahead with that terrorist summit?"

"Apparently," said the chief.

"I don't get it. I could lay waste to their country anytime I wanted and they're taunting me. Their reaction to the Speedway bombing was appalling and despicable. And, now they're gathering the enemies of America in their capital? Unbelievable."

"They think we'll never attack them."

"Why? Because our media declares they'd be hard to beat. They had better stop listening to the pundits. We learned a lesson in Iraq. After the ass-whipping stops, we're out of there. There will be no more rebuilding countries under my administration. They are on their own to pick up the pieces," said the president.

The first lady liked being outside. There wasn't a TV for her husband to shout at, so maybe there would be a little peace at dinner tonight. But just then the chief asked, "Speaking of Iran, did you hear what Milton Fryer said about the Israeli nuclear weapons?"

"Yeah, that was quite a yarn he was spinning."

The first lady said, "I know what you think about Milton Fryer, but I kind of like him."

"Apparently you're not alone," said the chief, as he was moved aside to let the wait staff serve him his dinner.

"You have to hand it to him, he did an excellent job following the Daytona attack, and I've never seen a person handle the media the way he does. They love him. It's a good thing that he isn't calling for my impeachment."

The first lady looked thoughtful and then said, "It would be good if we took one of his suggestions."

"Are you kidding? Which one of his crazy notions do you suggest?"

"The ban on Sunday driving to save fuel might be workable."

"Didn't we try that following the oil embargo during the Jimmy Carter Administration?"

The chief of staff said, "Yeah, it was totally unworkable with all the exceptions, but it made people feel that the government was doing something."

"Doesn't have much pizzazz."

"But a ban on private jets sounds good. Make the celebrities take public transportation. The voters would eat that up."

"Okay, we'll do that. Get somebody to suggest it tomorrow and I'll accept it."

"What does Milton have to say about Diaz in South America?"

"He says we should assassinate him."

"Isn't that the second time one of our Christian brothers called for his assassination?"

"I believe so," said his wife.

"Tell me, at the time, was I for it or against it?" asked the president with a straight face."

The first lady said, "You were against it, dear."

"And why was that, my sweetie?"

"Because your sister's husband works as a lobbyist for his country's oil company."

"Ouch."

47

THE PRESIDENT WOKE UP to the sound of rain at the Camp David compound. That's just great, he thought; things aren't depressing enough. It was early, so the Sunday morning news shows wouldn't be on for several hours. In the meantime, he would catch up on some reading. First, he'd see if he could wrestle up a cup of coffee. When he went into the kitchen, he found the attorney general, who in the president's opinion had been acting strange for the last few weeks. He thought that maybe the strain of the last several months was getting to him. The president figured he could do his reading another time, so he asked the attorney general if something was wrong.

A half hour later, the Secret Service went into full alert status. They heard yelling and quite a commotion coming from the kitchen area. The agents arrived as the president was pushing the attorney general through the back door. The two were now standing in the rain when the president asked, "How long have you known about this?"

"About four weeks, Mr. President."

"Why haven't you told me before?"

"We were double-checking the FBI team's findings. We were also looking for other links to the Iranians."

"Don't you realize what this means?"

"That's why we wanted to be sure we got it right."

The first lady stuck her head out the back door. "What are you two doing standing in the rain?" Her secret service agent woke her and told her about the commotion, so she had come over to see what was going on. As soon as she saw her husband's face, she backed off and told one of the secret service agents to find the chief of staff.

Moments later, the chief of staff met the president as he was heading for the conference room. "Find me the Defense secretary," the president bellowed.

The president had ordered that he not be disturbed, and it had been an hour since the he locked the Defense secretary and his chief of staff in the conference room. By now, the whole Camp David compound was buzzing with speculation.

"That's all the details I can give you, Mr. President. That's all I know," said the attorney general.

The president cancelled all his meetings for the day and flew back to Washington. He swore the secretary of Defense and the attorney general to secrecy. He gave them a number of tasks, and they were to report to him the following day.

48

THE FBI DIRECTOR had summoned Rob Jamison, Beth Cuddy and Mark Siene to Washington. They were told only that an independent team of agents had confirmed Mark's findings. Since air travel was difficult with the shortage of aviation fuel, Mark had to take an earlier flight. Now Beth and Rob were together as they waited in the departure area.

"I don't get it."

"Beth, please give it a rest."

"What in the world could you possibly see in her? You yourself said that she's manipulative, shallow and untrustworthy."

"Will you ever let this go? You've been on me for weeks about this. I should've taken the flight with Mark."

"Well, you've never given me an answer."

"And I owe you an answer because . . .?"

"We were partners for two and half years and you deceived me the whole time. If the public ever found out what she did, she'd be the most hated women in America."

Rob thought that was a good point. He guessed this was where he should defend Sheryl by saying something inane about everyone making mistakes, but he wasn't going to do that with Beth. So instead, he said, "I don't believe I deceived you. Do you tell me about the men you sleep with?" As soon as he said it, he knew he had made a mistake. He expected her to pounce on him but she didn't. Instead, she just looked sad.

Beth Cuddy was angry with her ex-partner for weeks after learning about his secret relationship with Sheryl. She knew her anger was way out of proportion for the situation. It wasn't until now that she realized the reason was jealousy. She was jealous of Sheryl. "Why do men make such bad choices when it comes to women," she thought. Another woman at this point probably would have left it alone, but that was not Beth's way, so she started in at Rob again. She had to know. "Rob, you can't tell me after four years it's only the sex."

Rob didn't want to examine the reasons he was with Sheryl, so he said, "What difference does it make to you?"

"I have to know why you would want to be with a woman like that."

As far as Rob was concerned, discussing his feelings ranked somewhere among being poor, dead or going to the ballet. He knew Beth wasn't going to let it go, so he tried to explain it. "Why am I with Sheryl? Because she's needy. Sheryl's a train wreck ready to happen. I'm needed. I hate talking about these things. If you were a guy you'd understand."

"So you think she needs saving?"

"Don't you?"

"That can't be all of it."

"No, that's not all of it." Rob continued. "Present company excepted, most people disappoint me. Every time I get close to someone, they do something inconsiderate or worse. Sheryl will never disappoint me."

This last statement Beth could not understand and said, "Sheryl always disappoints everyone."

"That's the point. With Sheryl, I've set the bar so low, she could never do anything that would surprise me. It's almost fun to watch what she'll do next."

Beth thought Rob had truly lost his mind.

"She's just so wrong for you."

"And, who's right for me?" he said as their flight was called, which ended their conversation. Their seats were not together for the trip to Washington and Rob was glad.

After landing, they made their way directly to the Hoover Building. Mark was already in the lobby waiting. "There's been a change of plans. I was told by the director's executive assistant to wait here for instructions."

"That's it?" asked Rob.

"She asked me if I had a copy of the presentation I made last time we were here, which I do."

"I guess we'll just wait," said Rob.

A few minutes later another team of agents arrived. Apparently, when they called upstairs, they were told the same thing. Nobody was in the mood to mingle, so the two groups stayed apart from one another. A little while later a uniformed person walked up with a clipboard and asked their names. He then ushered the six out to a waiting Chevrolet Suburban that didn't look like a Bureau car. It resembled those heavy vehicles used by the Secret Service.

Mark, who was sitting next to Rob, asked, "Where do you think they're taking us."

"The White House."

Mark thought Rob was trying to be funny when, after a short ride, they were admitted to the White House grounds. An aide greeted them and asked them to follow her. She led the group to a West Wing conference room. She said, "This is the Cabinet Room. Who has the PowerPoint presentations?"

Mark and a member of the other team indicated they had. She pointed to a laptop computer on the long table and asked them to load the presentations. When they were finished, she told them that if they were hungry, there would be a light dinner provided in one of the smaller dining rooms.

Before they sat down to eat, the group introduced themselves, but there was little conversation at dinner. They did remark that the food was excellent, and if nothing else happened that night, at least someday they could tell the story about the night they had dinner at the White House. What they didn't know was that would only be an obscure detail of what was to follow.

After dinner they headed back to the Cabinet Room and were surprised to find the president alone watching the television monitors. He introduced himself, as if they didn't know who he was. He shook hands and then asked each one their name and for a little background. He then invited them to sit.

The president of the United States began, "The other day I was given some disturbing news by the attorney general. It was so disturbing, in fact, that I told him I wanted to hear it from the source. So I don't want you to pull any punches. Don't filter anything for my benefit. The reason you don't see anyone else here is that I want to hear it without anyone feeling they're under pressure to say the right thing in front of their boss. Is that clear to everyone here?"

The president looked at each person individually, and they all said, "Yes, Mr. President."

"Special Agent Siene, I was told that you were the first person to discover a connection to certain individuals. Is that correct?"

"I believe so, sir."

"I would like a first hand account of what you found."

Mark presented his findings as he had a month earlier. Only this time the president asked for details about his methods and the timeline of his discoveries. He also asked Beth and then Rob about their confidence level concerning Mark's findings. They answered that they both supervised Mark and could confirm he followed the proper protocol. The president went through the same ritual with the other FBI team, which confirmed Mark's findings.

"Is this the first time you've heard the presentation from each other?"

"Yes, Mr. President," they all responded.

"Have you heard anything here today that brings up a question?"

They paused for a few seconds, and then Rob said, "Sir, the business with Kasra Khatani being paid by the Iranians, we did not discover that."

"Thank you, I understand. I would like you to spend the night in Washington and return here tomorrow to make a presentation to my National Security Council and possibly the entire Cabinet."

"Yes, Sir"

The president went over to a little desk in the corner, opened the drawer and took out a deck of cards. The group collectively wondered what he was doing. The president shuffled the deck and dealt each person a card face down. As he was leaving he said, "High card gets to sleep in the Lincoln bedroom."

Rob and Beth both drew aces.

49

THE NEXT MORNING the president was in the
Oval Office. He had a lot to think about. The FBI's
case was compelling, and had no doubt that at least
some of the Iranian government officials had prior
knowledge of the Daytona attack. As a former prosecutor, he knew the term was depraved indifference for
letting people die when they could have been saved. It
was a crime. The question in his mind was not whether
they should be punished—that was a given, but how
and where—was the dilemma he faced. At some point,
the American people would find out about the Iranian's
conduct and would call for justice and he must respond.
In a few minutes, his National Security Council would
meet in the Cabinet room. The president knew the FBI
team had just briefed them. They would not have time
to decompress and emotions would be running high.
He had to be the voice of reason, but at this point, he
didn't feel like being reasonable.

His chief of staff knocked gently and told him it was time, so he followed him to the Cabinet room. The faces and body language told the story. He supposed that the other 300 million Americans would be striking a similar pose as they learned about the Iranian government's involvement in the attack. The president said, "The question before us is whether the Iranians knew about the attack in advance and just did nothing, or if they were involved in the planning and/or execution. You would agree the answer to that question would determine, in a large part, about the severity of our response—and make no mistake, there will be a response. The president slammed his palm on the table to punctuate the last point.

The president could see that every member of the National Security Council was anxious to have his/her say. However, before they began, the president said, "Mr. Vice President, I would like you to step out."

Without a word, the VP picked up his papers and left.

"Would anyone else like to leave?"

Everyone stayed. The group speculated that the president might discuss options that would be extra-legal, a euphemism for acts potentially illegal under United States law. By asking him to leave, the vice president would be free of any prosecution, and could ensure the continuity of the administration. The question of *what did he know, and when did he know it* would not be a problem for him.

"I believe the evidence presented by the FBI, clearly shows that a least seven members of the Iranian Ruling

Council had prior knowledge of the attack and profited from it. Does anybody have any issues with the FBI's conclusion or methods of attaining the information?" The president looked at each member and no one spoke up. "So we proceed with the assumption of guilt on the Iranians' part. Would that be a valid way to frame the remainder of the meeting?"

They all nodded again, so the president went on, "We will not let their evil deeds go unpunished. Everything is on the table. Who would like to speak first?"

The chairman of the Joint Chiefs of Staff said, "Mr. President, I believe the secretary of Defense has briefed you on our current readiness. Would you like me to share that information with the rest of this group before you entertain any suggestions?"

"Thank you, I think that would be helpful as well as enlightening," the president said, thinking about his briefing at Camp David. When the general was finished, the group looked disgusted.

"As I said before, all options are on the table, but given our present military situation, the viability of some would be in question. Who would like to begin?"

Two hours later, they had not reached any consensus on what the United States's response should be. As the president suspected the Defense secretary was hawkish on the matter and the secretary of State was much less enthusiastic about a full-bore attack. Since they weren't getting very far, the president called for a fifteen-minute break. He told his chief of staff to have the FBI team brief the remainder of his Cabinet as soon as possible. The president then turned on the TV monitors.

Three of the cable news networks were all working the same story. The Iranians were going ahead with their anti-American summit. They had invited everyone on the list of the U.S. State Department terrorist organizations except the Irish Republican Army. The Iranians were claiming that delegations representing each of these organizations had accepted the invitation. They had also invited anyone who was against America, *the Great Satan,* to a rally held on July 4th beginning at afternoon prayers and ending at sunset.

By now, most other members of the National Security Council watched alongside the president. There were interviews with correspondents in Tehran who were saying that the Iranians expected over a million people to attend. They were privately bragging that every enemy of the United States would be journeying to the Iranian capital. The commentator asked the reporter, "Have you heard about any Western leader who's planning to attend the rally?"

The reported answered, "A high-placed Iranian official hinted that Diaz from South America planned to attend."

The president heard the secretary of State say, "That bastard!"

"What's the thinking in other capitals of the region?" the commentator asked.

"Of course, no one really knows what the Iranian leaders are up to. However, the speculation is that this is an attempt to unite the various factions of the Sunni and Shiite religious groups. We have reports of radical

Muslims coming from all parts of the world, all professing to be enemies of America."

"Do you think the Iranian estimates of over a million people attending the rally are accurate?"

"I do. However, there is no way to tell. As you know, all Western media has been ordered to shut down their operations at least three days preceding the rally and ordered to leave the county."

The president turned off the monitors and sat down.

The secretary of State said, "Mr. President, I have an idea."

50

NATHAN NIBLOCK FINISHED his top-to-bottom internal review of the Threat Identification and Classification System and waited to talk to the admiral about his findings. It had taken almost four months, because Nathan wanted to be thorough. However, he could see that his boss, the admiral, was anxious to hear the results. Nathan knocked on the admiral's door jam.

"Is this a good time?"

"Sure, come on in."

"Admiral, as you know, TICS was developed to ensure that something like the Daytona incident wouldn't happen. In other words, it was a way to make sure all the intelligence services worked together to connect the dots. Obviously, that didn't happen. We did a complete review on the assumption that the system was flawed in some way. That was our premise."

"I'm glad you took that tack. I was afraid we would be susceptible to the normal Washington ass-covering.

So you tried to prove it was the system that was broken?"

"Yes, sir"

"Did you succeed?"

"I'm glad to report we failed miserably." Nathan said
with a smile. "We looked at every piece of information,
including that gleaned by open source as well as covert
operations. We looked at every party involved in the
Daytona conspiracy and it appears that nothing was
missed."

"What about the recipients of the information?"

"That was a whole different story, Admiral. When
we reconstructed the *who knew what when scenario*, it
appears that in hindsight, the information we provided
could have been used to possibly prevent the attack."

"Did you come to this conclusion yourself?"

"No, Admiral, I actually had to turn the investigation
over to my second in command because of a conflict of
interest I discovered."

"Can you elaborate?"

"Well, sir, to my surprise, one of the recipients turned out to be my ex-wife, who was a supervisor in the
FBI and a principal player in the investigation."

"I would say you're correct. It would've been a conflict. Did you know she worked for the FBI?"

"No, Admiral, I hadn't heard from her in over ten
years."

"So the conclusion that the failure to prevent the attack was caused by human error was, in fact, determined by someone other than yourself?"

"Yes, sir. It was a consensus opinion from the eight-person team from my area that did the investigation. There were no dissenters, I was told."

"What is your recommendation?"

"Continue to use the system as it was designed."

"I agree; no action is required by this agency. I would assume there is nothing in writing on your findings."

"There is no record on paper or kept digitally. All meeting notes have been destroyed."

"Thank you, Nathan."

After leaving the admiral's office, Nathan Niblock thought that it had gone well. He was sure, though, that the admiral had other teams who had made the same inquiries and had come to the same conclusion. Otherwise, there would have been more questions. Nathan knew that the TICS system performed flawlessly and the error was due to some human element. The fact that his ex-wife was involved up to her ears in the matter didn't surprise him. He told the truth to the admiral. He hadn't known she worked for the FBI and hadn't seen her since shortly after she graduated with her law degree. He was surprised that she kept her married name though.

Nathan checked his voice mail, which had a message from Mitch Sterling, his best friend and co-owner of a sailboat they kept on the Chesapeake. He had some free time, so he called him back. When his friend answered he said, "Hey, Mitch, what's up?"

"Are we still on for this Saturday? Weather's supposed to be good—10 to 15 knot easterly wind."

"Wouldn't miss it."

"While I have you on the phone, do you know any-one at the FBI who might talk to me?"

Mitch Sterling had been Nathan's roommate for three years at the Naval Academy. Mitch had worked on the *Trident*, which was the official newspaper of the Naval Academy. When he graduated, he was assigned a billet with the American Forces Press Service at the Pentagon. Nathan knew that Mitch had made a number of good contacts and when Mitch's naval service was com-pleted, the *Washington Post* snapped him up, no doubt because of his Rolodex. "What are you working on?" asked Nathan.

"My editor assigned me to the Daytona attack story to find out if it could have been prevented."

Nathan thought that was a coincidence. Naturally, he wasn't sharing anything he knew. His friend under-stood that as well. Nathan also knew the Washington press corps was getting stonewalled by the FBI, so they had been pulling out all the stops to find out what had happened. There were plenty of rumors, but so far no hard news about potential malfeasance. Nathan argued with himself whether he should tell his friend about Sheryl. He thought why not. The FBI didn't classify its roster of field office personnel. "Mitch, do you remem-ber my ex-wife, Sheryl?"

"Who could forget Sheryl?"

"I heard she works in the Jacksonville FBI field office as a special agent."

"Really? Are you kidding me? That's the office re-sponsible for the Daytona Beach area."

"I believe you're right."

"Hey, I owe you a big one."

"You can wash the boat down on Saturday."

"Deal."

Nathan knew he shouldn't have done it. But maybe his friend would come up with something that could help the Agency.

51

MITCH STERLING WAS AMAZED at his luck. No other reporter had ever gotten nearly this far. He had a name, but Mitch was also surprised that his friend Nathan had given it to him. He wasn't going to waste any time, so he found the number for the Jacksonville FBI Field Office on their website and called. When the receptionist answered, he asked to speak to Sheryl Niblock. There was a delay and then the receptionist said, "I'm sorry, sir, we don't have anyone by that name in our office. I checked our master listing and there isn't a listing for a Sheryl Niblock at the Bureau. Mitch thought that was strange. "I was told that she was a special agent in your office."

"No sir, I've never met her."

"Have you been working there long?"

"Yes sir, about four months."

Being a good reporter, he kept asking questions until the person stopped answering. "So you were there during the attack in Daytona?"

"No sir, I started just after."

"I'm an old friend of Sheryl's and I'd like to locate her. Is there someone else I can speak to who maybe has been there a little longer?"

"Hold on, sir. I'll connect you with one of our special agents."

Mitch waited about two minutes and then heard. "This is Special Agent Cuddy. How may I help you?"

"Yes, Special Agent, I was trying to locate another agent by the name of Sheryl Niblock."

"What is your name, sir?"

"Mitch Sterling."

"Well, Mr. Sterling, former assistant special agent in charge, Sheryl Niblock has left the Bureau."

"Do you have a phone number for her?"

"I'm sorry, sir. We don't make that information available."

"Okay, thank you."

Mitch thought that was strange. He was sure his buddy couldn't be wrong, so he set about to do some skip-tracing. He first tried to Google Sheryl by name. No luck, so he began looking in the online phone directories—no listings in the Jacksonville area. Then he tried public records, if she owned property, sometimes the county would have that information in its online tax rolls. Mitch got a hit; a Sheryl Niblock had recently sold property in the county. Now he had an address. Mitch went back to Google and entered the address.

The search engine returned three pages of possibilities, mostly real estate company websites. He picked one, located a phone number, then called. When the person answered, Mitch asked to speak to the realtor who handled the property at the address he had found on the Internet. They gave Mitch the realtor's cell phone number. He called and when she answered, Mitch told her he was an old friend who lost track of Sheryl and was trying to find her. The agent was skeptical at first, but Mitch described her. "She's tall, has auburn hair, green eyes and can be bitchy."

The realtor recognized Sheryl's description, so she gave him the number she had. Mitch called.

"Hello."

"Is this Sheryl?"

"Yes."

"This is Mitch Sterling. I don't know if you remember me, but I was at the Naval Academy with your ex-husband."

"I'm sorry, I don't remember the name."

"Well, I'm with the *Washington Post*, and we are looking into the events leading up to the Daytona Speedway attack."

"I don't know anything about that."

"Sheryl, didn't you work in the Jacksonville FBI field office at the time of the attack? I talked to them. I spoke with a Special Agent Cuddy."

Sheryl thought, "That bitch Beth Cuddy gave me up . . ."

"Listen, I have no comment."

Mitch could tell he was onto something. "Sheryl, you know the information will come out eventually. Somebody's going to spin it. I'm giving you a chance here to tell me your side."

Sheryl didn't know what to do. She thought the FBI would use her as a scapegoat. She was definitely going to look bad. "What did Beth Cuddy tell you?"

Mitch now was sure that he had something. "I really don't want to divulge information from a source. I think you can understand that." he said, knowing he was being somewhat deceitful. Mitch took a big chance and said. "I know you left the FBI the day after the attack. Why were you terminated?"

"I wasn't fired, I resigned. Did Beth Cuddy tell you I was fired?"

"Sheryl, why don't you just tell me what happened."

"If Milton Fryer had heeded my warning none of this would've happened. By the way that's off the record."

Mitch thought it was too late to go off the record and said, "Are you telling me that you warned Congressman Fryer that the Speedway might be attacked?"

"He wasn't a congressman then, he was the mayor."

Mitch thought this was unbelievable. Sheryl Niblock just confirmed that the FBI knew about the attack beforehand and had warned the city officials. This was Pulitzer material. "How was the mayor warned?"

Sheryl started thinking that maybe she had already said too much, but she wasn't going to let the FBI put it all on her. She wanted to talk to Rob before she said anything else. "That's all I have to say right now."

"Thank you, Sheryl. I'll be calling back." When Mitch hung up, he sat there and reflected on what he heard. Congressman Milton Fryer, the media star, was warned about the Daytona Speedway attack before it happened. Mitch got up and walked to his editor's office with his notes. He explained to his editor what he had—and, for the first time since he worked at the *Post*, he saw his editor smile. "Well, well. That horse's ass Milton Fryer with all his crazy talk is going down."

His editor told Mitch he was the primary on the story, but was assigning five more reporters. "This will be the second biggest story of the year," he told him. Mitch knew his editor didn't care for Milton at all. It had nothing to do with Milton's views. Apparently, a frequent guest on one cable network was a *Washington Post* reporter who Milton had savaged on national TV. The network scheduled the same reporter with Milton Fryer on a cable news show this very night. After several meetings between Mitch, his editor and senior *Post* management, a strategy for confronting Milton was decided. The reporter would lay back and at the end of the segment, she would ambush Milton with what they knew.

Later that day, the cable news show was going as expected. There was Milton against three other guests, including the *Post*'s reporter, and Milton was winning. He was talking about his plan to save fuel by banning Sunday driving, citing the biblical reference of Sunday being a day of rest. It was almost time for the segment to end when the *Washington Post* reporter asked the host, "Chris, do you think I could ask the congressman a question?"

"Sure, go ahead."

"Congressman Fryer, a former FBI official has told the *Washington Post* that you were warned beforehand about the Daytona Speedway attack. Is that true?"

The host felt sure Milton would skewer the reporter for asking such an outrageous question. Instead, Milton hesitated before he answered. "I wouldn't have exactly called it a warning."

The panel went nuts. The feeding frenzy was on. The host said, "You were told there would be an attack?"

"Well, no. Not like what happened."

"But you were told some kind of attack was possible?"

"What do you mean by the word—possible?"

"You were contacted by the FBI?"

"Well, I did have a conversation with a low ranking member of the Bureau."

"What was said in the conversation?"

"As I recall, it had something to do with the nearby airport."

Everybody watching the show could tell he was being evasive and maybe possibly even lying. "Was there any mention of the Daytona Speedway?"

"I don't recall."

"How could you not recall something like that?"

"It was month's ago."

"Congressman, it's not like we are asking you to recall your childhood. This was the biggest attack our country has ever seen. Surely, you would remember a conversation you had with the FBI?"

Milton looked at his watch. The show would be over in less than a minute. The host said, "Ladies and gentlemen, I've just been told by my producer that we will extend our program into the next hour. Please stay tuned."

Every network executive was now on the studio set, standing just off camera. Others had begun to arrive to watch this stunning turn of events. One of the nation's heroes was going down! No doubt about it, this was huge!

52

S THE YOUNG AIDE watched the members of
the Iranian Ruling Council take their seats, he
thought there would be no shooting the messenger
today. He was delivering good news. The protest rally
they organized was going well beyond anyone's expectations. At last count, nearly one million people from
nearly every radical Muslim group in the world had
descended on Tehran. Buses and trains from surrounding Middle Eastern countries were still arriving carrying demonstrators for today's activities. Others were
arriving by air from forty other countries not in the
region.

"I can tell by your face, you bring us good news,"
said the chief commander, thinking one would have to
be blind and deaf not to know their plan has been a
one-hundred percent success.

"Yes, sir. It is far beyond everyone's expectations.
The streets are crowded with foreigners. Business in the

shops is brisk and everyone seems very happy with the arrangements."

"Are all our guests getting along?"

"So far there have been no reports of violence among the different groups."

"That in itself could be seen as a miracle," said a council member, thinking that in another time and place many of these people would be shooting and blowing up each other."

"Their hatred for America and Israel far outweighs their internal political disagreements."

"Are all the groups on the American's list of terrorist organizations represented?"

"All twenty-eight of the Islamic organizations are here, as well as a few others."

"Excellent."

"So tell us, what is the agenda for today?"

"More speeches, sir—not that anyone is really listening though."

"Oh, my dear young friend, there are many, many people listening. They are just not in Tehran. We are sending a loud and clear message that Iran is now the real leader in the region. The world will have to deal with us."

"Has there been any response from the West?" asked another council member.

"No, sir. The foreign minister reports not even hearing a whisper of protest."

"They see how powerful we are. They will get rid of the ridiculous sanctions against us and will break with the United States and Israel at the first excuse."

"And what of friends in exile?"

"They sent a message to the press condemning the rally as being provocative and dangerous for our Iran."

"They are weaklings. They talk much and say little."

"Our actions prove to our people we were right to take our country back from such cowards. They let Israel do anything they wished for decades. It's time to drive the Zionists into the sea."

"Yes, sir."

"What is the plan for today?" asked the chief commander.

"Formal ceremonies, as you know, will take place at the Azadi Sports Complex. Many have already started to gather there for this evening's activities. I'm told the Metro is jammed with foreigners and there is not a taxi to be had."

"What about security?"

"We have taken some precautions against violence. Obviously no weapons will be allowed and each organization has been pre-assigned a special area. Many will be in the stadium or on the grounds surrounding it, but we've arranged for some of the more belligerent groups to be seated in the various halls with additional security. This way we can keep them apart and avoid any unpleasantness."

"Where will the Ruling Council be located?"

"A covered dais has been erected in the center of the field with seats for about twenty. I believe we will be able to accommodate at least 100,000 inside the stadium."

"How many people are estimated to attend?"

"I'm told that there are over 250,000 souls there already. I would not be surprised to see over a million by time you arrive this evening."

"Very good."

"Have all the foreign press left the country?"

"I believe so. We've shut down their bureaus and are jamming signals to there communications satellites. All video of the gathering will be edited before distribution to the world media."

"What is the schedule?"

"I've taken the liberty of preparing this," said the aide, passing out a one-page summary. "Please let me know if you would like any changes. As you can see, all activities culminate at sunset with the evening prayers."

"Very well."

53

AIR FORCE MAJOR PAUL PALENA was sitting in the ready room thinking about what a bad year it had been. First, his brother was killed in the Daytona attack and then he was stationed in the middle of nowhere. When they assigned him to the B-2 Stealth Bomber program, the aircraft were all flown out of Whiteman Air Force Base in Missouri. Since he grew up in Kansas City, where his family still lived, it was perfect. He remembered hearing a rumor that the Pentagon was moving two of the B-2 Spirit bombers to Guam, which turned out to be true. He was thankful the Air Force hadn't chosen him. But then he found out that two more crews would be sent to Diego Garcia in the Indian Ocean. He thought that at least there were cities on Guam. There was absolutely nothing here, and he was miserable. The major was one of two pilots assigned to a B-2 bomber named Spirit of Florida. Major

Palena was the aircraft commander and sat in the left seat. He listened to his mission commander, the other pilot on the two-man flight crew, go back and forth with a couple of Navy flyers who had arrived the night before in their Super Hornets. They were on their way to rendezvous with their carrier. Naturally, they were arguing about whose branch of service had the best pilots.

"I'd like to see you make a carrier landing at night."

"What do you mean, landing? They catch you with a big rubber band. You Navy guys always arrive late and leave early. We're kicking ass while you jack-offs are still in your bunks."

"When we fight, it's up close and personal. You people sneak in with your billion-dollar giant boom-a-rang and sneak out again. I hear you even have a bathroom and shower in those flying RVs."

"At least we don't have to piss our pants like you guys."

The repartee continued for some time until one of the Navy pilots asked Paul if he could see his aircraft. He never saw a B-2 up close. The major figured it was something to do, so they headed outside to the hanger. On the way, a giant C-5A cargo plane was taxiing up to an unloading area while another aircraft, a Gulfstream C-37A, was landing. The C-37A was the military version of a long-range business jet. They normally carried VIPs and high-ranking officers.

While they were showing the Navy pilots the stealth bomber, a blue tug pulling a covered trolley with what looked like two long bombs was heading toward their aircraft. An Air Force sergeant walked up to them.

"I'm sorry, sirs. I have to ask you to leave the building for a while."

One of the Navy pilots asked, "What's that about?"

"I have no idea," said the major. "Have you guys heard about anything going on?"

"No," they said as they went back into the ready room. Later, the pilots were back harassing each other when one Navy flyer called, "Attention on deck!"

Standing there in the doorway was a two-star general. "As you were." He looked at the Navy pilots and said, "Will you gentlemen excuse us?"

"Yes, sir."

The general said, "Please sit down. Are you the crew of AV-17 or AV-1?"

"AV-17, sir."

"Good, the Spirit of Florida has a mission."

The major thought this is unusual, a mission briefing given by a two-star and said, "Would you like me to get the Spirit of America crew."

"No Major, only one aircraft is needed for this mission."

The general started his briefing. "Your call sign will be Liberty Bell. You'll be wheels up at 1400 hours. For now, all you need to know is that you'll be flying a heading of 3-5-7 degrees. Four hours out, you will be vectored by AWACS, call sign Chalice, to your refueling coordinates and then to your target."

"Yes, sir."

"Are you gentlemen familiar with MOAB?"

His mission commander asked, "The Mother of All Bombs?"

"Yes, Lieutenant, Massive Ordinance Air Blast Bomb, what do you know about it?"

"Sir, I know it won't fit in our aircraft. It was designed to be dropped from a transport plane. It's an air blast bomb. Supposedly it can destroy nine city blocks, and it produces a mushroom cloud similar to an atomic device, that's why we choose not to use it."

"That's all correct, Lieutenant, except for one item, the size. A new design reduces the dimensions along with some of its power to fit into your B-2. You'll be carrying a pair to your destination. The combined affect of both bombs dropped simultaneously, is estimated to be equivalent to 12 city blocks of total destruction."

The major thought, "Holy crap."

"Any questions, gentlemen?"

The major had a ton of questions, but he knew the general wouldn't answer any of them.

"Good luck."

Immediately, the flight crew of the Spirit of Florida went to their aircraft which was readied for departure. They watched from the taxiway as the Gulfstream carrying the general took off. Their take-off turned out to be a little dicey because of all the weight they were carrying. The aircraft was just below its safe operating limits. They did as instructed. The crew had been flying the assigned heading for about four hours when they heard, "Liberty Bell, this is Chalice, over."

The major thought that must be AWACS. "Chalice, Liberty Bell."

"Liberty Bell, change heading to 3-5-5 degrees."

"Roger, Liberty Bell"

After a few seconds, the mission commander said, "I think we're going to Iran."

A minute later, "Liberty Bell, this is Chalice."

"Go ahead, Chalice."

"Prepare for GPS and weapon system downloads."

"Roger, Chalice."

The major could see that the other pilot was excited. "Are we going to Iran?"

"Yes we are . . . Tehran."

Now the Major knew where they were going and what they were carrying. This would be his first combat mission, but he wasn't really that nervous until he heard the next transmission from AWACS. "Liberty Bell, this is Chalice."

"Go ahead, Chalice."

"Prepare for message from POTUS"

The two pilots looked at each other. "It sounded like he said POTUS."

The major called AWACS. "Please say again, last."

"Liberty Bell, prepare for message from POTUS."

The major thought wow; POTUS, the President of the United States, wanted to speak with them.

"Liberty Bell, this is POTUS."

"Liberty Bell."

"Major, this is the president. Let's dispense with the normal radio protocol. All our transmissions will be recorded in plain English from now on. I know your names, but I won't use them."

"Yes, sir."

"You will get your orders from me directly. Do you understand?"

"Yes, Mr. President."

"When you are exactly 13 minutes from your target, please call me. I'll be standing by. At thirty seconds from the target, I want you to contact me again for your orders. Is that understood?"

"Yes, Mr. President."

The pilots heard nothing for the next hour until the AWACS contacted them again for their rendezvous with the tanker that would refuel them, and then there were no transmissions after that. At 14 minutes, the mission commander said, "Contact with the president is in 45 seconds." After counting down the time, the major called "POTUS, this is Liberty Bell."

"Go ahead, Major."

"We are 13 minutes from target."

"In a few minutes you will hear me address the American people. By the way, I was sorry to hear about your brother."

"Thank you, Mr. President."

"If I'm still speaking when you're 30 seconds from your target, I want you to interrupt me. Do you understand?"

"Yes, Mr. President."

After a few minutes the B-2 bomber crew heard the president's voice addressing the nation.

54

IT WAS JULY 4TH and late morning on the East
Coast. Most people were at home because of the
holiday. Unlike the Independence Day festivities of the
years past with the parades and fireworks displays, this
year none of that was planned for many communities.
The American people didn't have much to celebrate,
and there was still a fear of gathering in large crowds.
The mood of the country could be described as dour.
Beth had even cancelled her big annual Fourth of July
cookout, where she invited her friends and co-workers
to her home. She had to admit to herself that this had
more to do with her not wanting to see Sheryl and Rob
together than anything to do with the fall-out from the
Speedway tragedy. Later on, she was going to Mark's to
join him and his family for a barbecue. It was a small
going-away celebration. The FBI was transferring him
to Washington, D.C. to organize and supervise a new
area. Mark would get his own section because of his

excellent work identifying the Iranians through their stock market transactions. The area would be used to possibly identify other terrorists in the same way. Beth had no doubt that someday Mark would be a special agent in charge of his own field office. He was definitely on the fast track.

She had just finished showering after her morning run and planned to work on the new kayak project that waited in her workshop. The TV was on a news station, but she wasn't paying much attention. Most of the news stories had to do with the FBI warning Milton Fryer about the attack. The usual *what was he told* was the theme of most of the coverage for the last week. Sheryl's name had come up several times, but the focus was mostly on Milton.

Then she heard, "Ladies and gentlemen, we are told that there is something going on at the White House."

Beth watched as the screen changed to a female reporter who was still trying to get herself settled. She looked up startled. Apparently the director was telling her in her earpiece that she was already on the air.

"Can you tell us what's happening over there?"

"This is what we know so far; the White House has asked the networks to provide air time for a message of national importance."

"Did they give any indication what it was about?"

"No, just that they would be sending us a feed and asking us to broadcast it."

A few seconds later, Beth saw the picture had changed. The president of the United States was standing in the center of a large room. Behind him were three huge monitors. In front of him were a number of military people sitting at their consoles.

"Is that NASA we're looking at, Vicky?"

"No, Steve. It appears to be a military command & control center of some kind. I've seen similar ones when I was reporting from the Persian Gulf."

"I think you're right."

"I don't hear any sound, do you?"

Then he heard the president begin speaking, "My fellow Americans, over two centuries ago, a group of brave men came together to declare our independence from the tyranny of oppressive government and to set forth the principles of a free people. Over the years, much blood has been shed, both on our native soil and in foreign lands, to protect our most valued ideals, those of liberty and freedom. We have fought and continue to fight for these things because they are more precious to us than peace. We have sacrificed our men and women for the principles that gave our nation its birth. And, each generation has learned that these ideals are not guaranteed, but must be earned.

There will always be those in the world who will try to impose their tyranny through aggression and terror, and we will fight them, no matter what the cost in blood or treasure. Therefore, to that end, today, the birthday of our great country, I bring before you a matter of immense importance to our nation. As you all know, we have recently suffered a tragedy beyond all reasoning—an attack on our people and an assault on our way of life. The forces against us will use any means to achieve their goal, which is the complete and total destruction of America and the principals for which she stands.

There are those in the world who say America is impotent now and no longer relevant. We have become weak and vulnerable. There are some, even in our own country, who echo these sentiments. Will I tell you now, they are wrong? As long as I am president of these great United States, I will do whatever it takes to protect our people from the evils of those organizations and governments who intend us harm.

My fellow Americans, the time for eulogies is over. The dead have been buried, but their families still suffer. The American people are dealing with hardships, some not seen since the Great Depression. Some World leaders have threatened us with further economic harm. Some are even gathering the enemies of the United States to celebrate our tragedy. I tell them now, you have made a grave mistake.

I, like all those presidents before me, swore an oath to protect our country against all enemies, foreign and domestic. This is the most important duty of this office. There has been much criticism for my lack of action after the devastating attack on our country. It was inconceivable to me that any government could have been involved in this heinous assault on our people. Well, my fellow Americans, I was wrong. We now have incontrovertible proof that certain members of the Iranian government had prior knowledge of the attack and profited from it. At this very moment, there are over one million of our enemies dedicated to the destruction of the United States gathered in Tehran. They have been invited by the same government officials who were involved in the Daytona attack."

As the president spoke, behind him the three monitors were showing disturbing images. To the president's right, video the public had originally seen that awful day from the airship was playing. To his left was the procession to the National Cemetery. Directly behind him, a KH-13 spy satellite was transmitting real time images showing the crowds at the Sports Complex in Tehran holding signs saying, *Death to America* and shaking their arms and fists.

The president continued, "To those leaders who helped perpetrate this evil deed, my message to you is simple. You have forfeited your lives. Your lack of humanity and compassion and your corruption makes you unfit to continue in this world." The president turned around and pointed to the monitor behind him. "And, to our enemies dedicated to the destruction of America and all she stands for, you will soon hear our ring of freedom."

The president continued looking at the monitor for about fifteen seconds, and then the American people heard, "POTUS, this is Liberty Bell."

The president hesitated for a second, then said, "Go ahead, Liberty Bell."

"Thirty seconds to target, Mr. President."

"Liberty Bell, make your weapons free—let our eagles fly . . ."

EPILOGUE

THE WORLD REACTED to the bombing of Tehran in a predictable way. Some countries enthusiastically supported it. Others condemned it as provocative and unnecessary. The United Nations response was reminiscent of its reaction when Israel bombed Iraq's nuclear installations in 1981—world leaders criticized it outright in their public pronouncements, but secretly were relieved that Israel did destroy the nuclear facilities. However, in the United States, the public wholeheartedly embraced the president's actions. His approval ratings hit an all time high for any American leader, and he handily won re-election.

International criticism was short lived, as the world saw a number of positive benefits, especially in the Middle East. Many of the more radical elements of their societies had disappeared. Lebanon's army, with the help of Israel, drove what remained of Hezbollah out of that country. In Palestine, much of Hamas was devastated in the attack on Tehran. The organization's West Bank and Gaza rivals easily prevailed in their ongoing feud, setting the stage for a peace treaty with Israel. This finally led to the Palestinians getting their own independent state. Those radicals in other Muslim countries, who had not gone to Tehran, curtailed the use of suicide bombings against each other after several terrorist groups adopted Milton Fryer's ideas on retribution. With the loss of public esteem for their acts, because of the fear of reprisals against their families, recruits for this despicable act became scarce. However, in its place were many more kidnappings.

Russian protestations against America's actions were uncharacteristically muted. This, no doubt, had something to do with their problems in Chechnya. Hostilities suddenly abated there. Apparently, the rebel leaders in that former Soviet region had attended the rally in Iran. They were not there so much to protest the United States as to make contacts for later weapons purchases. However, the result was the same.

China incited several incidents, which eventually led them to invade North Korea—deposing that notorious regime. Each side lost countless numbers of young men. For the Chinese government this had the beneficial effect in reducing the number of young single males in their country. The Chinese government also repopulated North Korea with some of their citizens. Chinese men immigrated there during the occupation, and many inter-married with the available Korean women.

With the neutralizing of North Korea, American military forces were free to leave the Peninsula. Taiwan, fearing a possible Chinese attack, held a referendum on whether they should join the mainland using the Hong Kong model. The measure, after narrowly passing, will take affect in 2030.

The former supreme leader of Iran, Ayatollah Kasmani, along with the Council of Guardians who had been exiled during the coups by the leaders of the Revolution Guards, returned without delay to govern their country. Iran's neighbors had closed their borders immediately following the Tehran attack, not allowing the survivors to leave. The Ayatollah Kasmani considered these foreigners as collaborators with the traitorous Revolutionary Guards' leaders. He vowed to treat their actions harshly. The Ayatollah later kept his word and executed thousands, almost all of them Sunnis. Meanwhile, the political environment in that country changed, allowing much of the Iranian populace to call for better relations with the United States. This, at the end of the day, led to détente with America, and Iran giving up its nuclear ambitions. However, Israel remained a favorite subject of their loathing and antipathy.

The South American dictator, so antagonistic to the United States, survived the attack and eventually made it out of Persia. However, in the meantime, a revolution occurred in his own country. He was deposed and now lives the life of luxury with stolen oil money in Paris. Petroleum from his country continues to flow to America.

On the home front, the requirement by Homeland Security for the police authorities to arrange escorts for all fuel trucks was rescinded. Within days, the supply of fuel was plentiful in all parts of the country, but the price didn't go down appreciably. However, the American people had learned to do more with less. It was a good thing since Congress and the Administration did little to reduce the dependence on foreign oil. Government and industry did finally abandon ethanol as a viable alternative to fossil fuels. Ethanol production slowly waned and food prices came down.

The pall that hung over the American public lifted, and people were back out enjoying themselves again. The city of Daytona Beach rebuilt the racetrack in its former location and once again was able to host *The Great American Race*. NASCAR honored those killed by automatically bringing out the *caution flag* on lap 121 of every race. The fans would stand in silence for that lap, in remembrance of their friends who had fallen on that awful day. The term *Lap 121*, much like the word *Katrina*, would become a euphemism when speaking about major tragedies.

The Canadian government refused to extradite Kasra Khatani because he faced the death penalty in America. He was convicted of murder and is serving five life sentences. The Canadians have him in solitary confinement because of several attempts on his life.

Milton Fryer resigned from Congress and went back to preaching. He is as popular as ever with his parishioners, and is still a frequent guest on many of the religious talk shows. However, most of the secular American public doesn't have much use for him or his ideas.

The FBI promoted Mark Siene to supervisory special agent soon after he arrived in Washington, D.C., where he set up a special unit. After a successful assignment there, the Bureau put him in charge of the FBI's legal attaché office in Brasilia, Brazil, where he is currently using his Portuguese language skills.

Sheryl Niblock passed the Florida Bar Exam is now a defense attorney in Palm Beach County. She married Rob Jamison's next-door neighbor, Mr. Moretti, who turned out to be a very wealthy man. He passed away less than a year after they married and left his entire fortune to Sheryl. Currently, there is a major court fight between Sheryl and Peter Moretti's children over the estate—his children claiming that Sheryl unduly manipulated him, a charge she denies.

Rob Jamison and Beth Cuddy, counting on the reputation of the White House staff for their discretion, did spend the night together in the Lincoln Bedroom. Rob left his temporary assignment at the FBI several months later and is now working as a private investigator.

Beth Cuddy, still with the FBI, married Rob Jamison, and they are now expecting their first child.

THE END

More? Visit www.Lap121.com

About the Author

Rob DiGiacomo, before writing his first novel was the author of numerous non-fiction articles that appeared in various trade magazines and newsletters. He spent his early years growing up in New England and attended the University of Rhode Island after serving in the United States Navy. He moved to Florida in 1989 and now resides in the Tampa Bay area where he's working on his next book.

E-mail him at: author@lap121.com

www.ingramcontent.com/pod-product-compliance
Lightning Source LLC
Chambersburg PA
CBHW050556260626
47157CB00002B/584